"What?" She said hostilely, bending down by the car to look at him fully.

"Good morning to you too, Arnella," Alric said. His voice was well modulated and sounded smooth, like a radio announcer's. *Does everybody who went to that university come out sounding refined*? she wondered.

"Morning," Arnella said. She couldn't keep the abrupt tone from her voice. Alric had avoided her for the past ten or so years. Why the sudden about face?

"So what grand adventure are you off to?" he asked, gazing at her lazily and then at her opened car trunk.

"Why do you care?" Arnella frowned. "And why are you suddenly talking to me?"

"I thought about it, and I concluded that nobody, not even you, could be as bad as you are made out to be; so I thought I would break the ice, you know, get to know you a bit better like a good neighbor should. I have listened to the gossip about you but realized that I've never once tried talking to you myself."

"Oh, heavens," Arnella sighed, "that sounds like guilty Christian charity talking. When did you decide to do this? You know what I think. I think you shouldn't talk to me in public and in broad daylight...

SENSE OF RUMOR

BRENDA BARRETT

JAMAICA TREASURES

SENSE OF RUMOR

Published by Jamaica Treasures
Kingston, Jamaica

This is a work of fiction. Names, characters, places, and incidents are either the product of the author's imagination or are used fictitiously. Any resemblance to an actual person or persons, living or dead, events, or locales is entirely coincidental.

ISBN - 978-976-8247-04-9
Jamaica Treasures Ltd.
P.O. Box 482
Kingston 19
Jamaica W.I.
www.fiwibooks.com

Other books in the Bancroft Family Series:

ALSO BY BRENDA BARRETT

Di Taxi Ride and Other Stories
The Pull of Freedom
The Empty Hammock
New Beginnings
Full Circle
The Preacher And The Prostitute
Private Sins (Three Rivers)
Loving Mr. Wright (Three Rivers)
Unholy Matrimony (Three Rivers)
If It Ain't Broke (Three Rivers)
Going Solo (New Song)
Duet On Fire (New Song)
Tangled Chords (New Song)
Broken Harmony (New Song)
A Past Refrain (New Song)
Perfect Melody (New Song)
Love Triangle: Three Sides To The Story
Love Triangle: After The End
Love Triangle: On The Rebound

ABOUT THE AUTHOR

Books have always been a big part of life for Jamaican born Brenda Barrett, she reports that she gets withdrawal symptoms if she does not consume at least two books per week. That is all she can manage these days, as her days are filled with writing, a natural progression from her love of reading. Currently, Brenda has several novels on the market, she writes predominantly in the historical fiction, Christian fiction, comedy and romance genres.

Apart from writing fictional books, Brenda writes for her blogs blackhair101.com; where she gives hair care tips and fiwibooks.com, where she shares about her writing life.

You can connect with Brenda online at:
Brenda-Barrett.com
Twitter.com/AuthorWriterBB
Facebook.com/AuthorBrendaBarrett

Chapter One

"What's up, Arnella? You good?" Cory waved to her from the other side of the pool where she was lounging, and winked.

Arnella ignored him. He had been pestering her to date him since high school days. Now that he was attending Mount Faith and entering second year of the Medical Technology program, he thought that he was a good catch. He could be, she supposed. He was cute in a nerdy kind of way. If only he didn't try so hard to get her to like him—that was a big turn off for her.

She adjusted her dark glasses and lay back in the floating donut. She was bored; it was the kind of boredom that was bone deep and fuelled from a lack of meaningful activity. Most of her friends, if she could call them that, had moved on from high school and were either in their second year of university or had found jobs which they constantly complained about.

She was doing nothing. Even Tracy, her only true friend in the world, whose birthday party she was attending, seemed as if she was moving on without her. Tracy had different friends and was talking more maturely. She didn't find Arnella as entertaining anymore. In the past, she was the one that Tracy looked to for advice. Now, Tracy rarely asked her for anything or about anything. She was in her second year at university now, and Arnella had been relegated to just her wild high school pal who she hung out with to spite her conservative parents.

She glanced around the poolside and could count, on one hand, the people here that were from Tracy's high school, there were Cory, David, and Jeff. They were the only three persons she knew from high school, and all three of them were now at Mount Faith. The other persons were Tracy's university friends.

Tracy's spacious backyard was full with them—Mount Faith people. Some were in the pool, and one or two of them had initiated conversations with Arnella, but she was self-conscious about being among strangers.

She glanced at her root beer bottle. She had lined them up at the poolside. She had had five beers, and now she was feeling tipsy. She thought Tracy had said that they were non-alcoholic. She didn't touch alcohol: not with her history.

"Hey, Nella," Tracy gestured to her from poolside. "He's here," she whispered fiercely. "Alric is here! What should I do?"

Arnella lazily lifted her glasses and stuck it in her hair, "Say hi, and stop acting like you like him."

Tracy had a panicked look on her face, as if she were going to expire. "I don't know how to do that thing you do."

"What thing?" Arnella squinted at her in the sunlight.

"The bored thing, the nothing can touch me thing."

Arnella laughed dryly, "My attitude comes from years of hard living and growing up with an alcoholic mother."

Tracy stood up and looked at her petite friend. "I can't believe that I have a handicap because I'm from a regular, happy nuclear family."

Arnella nodded, "It is a handicap. Regular families are so yesterday."

She laughed as Tracy shook her head in exasperation, then twisted around in her tube and spotted Tracy's crush.

He was standing near the makeshift bar with his hands covering his ears from the extremely loud party music. Arnella had warned Tracy that he was too straitlaced and stuck up for this crowd, but Tracy asked him to attend anyway: Alric Peterson, son of Pastor Peterson, the university's church pastor.

Tracy had dragged her to the university church one night to check him out, even though she had told her that she already knew Alric. He was the goofy kid who lived in the big house on her street in Fair Ridges, a suburban community on the outskirts of Santa Cruz.

According to Tracy, he had grown into his looks. She was right. Arnella could not reconcile his grown-up look with the image in her head of an awkward big-eared kid from her childhood days who used to ride past her house slowly and watch her with a smirk on his face.

She had lived at the top of the street in an old turn of the period house with an unkempt yard. It was the sore thumb on the block. Arnella could still remember the first time Alric said hi to her. She had just arrived in Jamaica and his parents had welcomed her mother to the neighborhood. His mother had baked a cake and handed them a tract to attend some crusade or the other.

Her mother hadn't been interested and the Peterson's didn't

reach out to them anymore. Alric and Arnella were like night and day in every way, including their social standing, so they had not managed to rub shoulders, even as children.

She looked him over, standing there now: tall, lean, and handsome. Somebody must have told him that a completely baldhead, coupled with that goatee, gave him a certain look. He was killing it. No wonder Tracy was jittery over him: he was very handsome. He was so not her type though—he was attending a pool party in dress pants and long sleeved shirt, though the light green shirt flattered his smooth nutmeg color nicely.

"Hey, Alric," Arnella shouted, wanting to see him squirm when he recognized who was calling to him. He looked around when he heard his name.

Arnella waved to him, and his eyes widened when he saw her. At first, she wasn't sure why he looked so shell-shocked then she realized that he was probably shocked at her half-naked state.

Her bikini was a caramel shade, just like her skin. The poor guy probably thought she was naked. She looked down at her chest and realized that her nipple ring was showing through her bikini top.

She shrugged. *If he has never seen a nipple ring before, too bad.* She decided to shock him even more and stick out her tongue. She had gotten it pierced just last month. It no longer felt sore, but she was yearning to stop wearing it. Like all her piercings, she had been making a statement. Her body was hers to do with as she pleased, and to hell with anybody else. She was planning to get tattoos next but was too scared of anybody putting inferior artwork on her body, given the high cost of getting tattoos removed.

Alric didn't move. Arnella Bancroft was calling to him in a friendly manner. He wasn't sure how to respond.

He had spent most of his life thinking of Arnella as Satan incarnate. The entire Fair Ridges neighborhood, where they lived, thought so too. Her mother had had a hard time reigning her in from she was little, and there were rumors and counter-rumors about Arnella that could fill a tome of books; most of those rumors were bad and portrayed her as being indecent. For instance, there was one rumor that she ran away, at age fourteen, and lived with a priest as his concubine, and another rumor that she had chain-smoked marijuana since she was eight. He wondered how she could still be alive.

Arnella got out of the pool and stretched, arching her back and showing off her belly ring with a skull on it. Her g-string bikini left little to the imagination. She was perfectly shaped, like a centerfold in one of those men's magazines, and was casual about her state of undress.

Her hair was loosely pinned up on top of her head; wet tendrils snaked down her back and clung to her skin like a kiss. From where he stood, he could see a birthmark on her shoulder.

Alric's eyes swiveled to Tracy, who was dressed in a more modest one-piece bathing suit. She was a more wholesome picture to look at in her full black ensemble. She didn't inspire thoughts of impurity in a man.

He had no idea why he had agreed to stop by Tracy's birthday party. His only excuse was that her house was on the way to Mount Faith and that he had work today. He knew Tracy liked him, but she had Arnella Bancroft as a friend; and that was a big turn off. It was Tracy's big fault, but his brain reminded him that Arnella was also Tracy's draw. He had always been interested in Arnella. She was like a fascinating train wreck. He wondered how Tracy tolerated her as a friend. How could anyone tolerate such a stubborn headstrong girl for long without being burned in the heat of her rebellion?

He almost resented the fact that her hard living was not showing on her face or her body. He glanced at her again. She had been a pretty little girl with a propensity to cuss like a fisherman, but now she was a beautiful woman with a killer body, who obviously was not afraid to show it off. Several persons, including women, had stopped to watch as she stretched. Some stares were filled with jealousy, others with pure lust.

He felt like grabbing a towel from somewhere to cover her up. She would have laughed at that. He remembered that she had an evil sounding cackle that irked him. Sometimes, when he was walking home from school, he would hear her laughing in her yard. It wasn't a laugh that indicated that she found something funny; it was just one of those evil sounds.

Though Tracy walked over to him and pulled him into a quiet area in a gazebo where the music wasn't pulsating in his chest, he found himself looking around for Arnella. *Where did she go?*

Then he spotted her with three men. She was talking to them and laughing at something one of them said. One with a buzz cut handed her a drink, and the next thing he knew, she was leaning into him and rubbing on him like a cat.

He felt unaccountably angry. "Why are you friends with Arnella?" he asked Tracy a bit too harshly when he saw what was taking place right there in Tracy's backyard.

She looked at him; her mouth opened slightly, a bit taken aback by his harsh demand. "I don't know; she is a nice person when you get to know her."

He watched as Arnella was hugged tightly by one of the other guys. The thin one with the buzz cut had let her go but was openly cupping one of Arnella's butt cheeks with one of his hands, caressing it and laughing at something that one of the other guys said.

"Can't you see what she is doing, in broad daylight, at your party?" he asked Tracy with incredulity.

Tracy frowned and took her time to look around. "What? I don't see her."

"Because she has gone off with those men," Alric shook his head, "maybe to a private room. She has no boundaries and no sense of decency, that girl. It's your house Tracy; you can't encourage that kind of thing."

Tracy was looking at him, a hint of displeasure crossing her features. "Those are our friends from high school. Arnella is not interested in young guys, and she is an adult. She can go wherever she wants to go and do whomever she wants to do."

"That may be true," Alric growled, "but I am a Christian. I don't just go to church. This type of lifestyle is not for me: free sex, booze, and do what you want because you can. Sorry!" He spun around, "I have to go. I'll see you around school next semester, okay."

"But, Alric," Tracy spread her arms, beseeching him to stay, "Arnella is not around anymore. See: she is not by the poolside. Why are you so upset?"

"Find out what she is doing in your house and stop it," Alric said, seething. Images of Arnella at this moment, having indiscriminate sex were enough to raise his blood pressure to heights he feared was not at all healthy.

He felt an irrational anger when Tracy shook her head.

"Seriously, Alric! She is an adult! I can't go around searching for her like I am some sort of mother hen."

"It's your house," Alric said. "Where are your parents?"

"Work," Tracy frowned. "Alric, please stay. The music is not that bad. I can't play Rock of Ages or Amazing Grace at my party, and it's not real alcohol. It's fake champagne and root beer."

Alric shook his head, "I have to go to work. See you around."

He cast his eye across the back of the building. There was a sliding glass door, which was heavily tinted and probably led to a changing room. That was probably where Arnella went with those guys. He was itching to go in there, and he almost did, but he thought about how ridiculous he would look; instead, he stormed off from the pool area and walked around to the side of the house, angrily brushing aside the overhanging hibiscus as he made his way to his car.

He still felt angry toward Arnella even when he was driving along the avenue and into the town of Santa Cruz.

It wasn't until he was making his way up to Mount Faith to his summer job as a lab instructor that he recognized that what he was feeling was jealousy. When he recognized it, he had to stop at the side of the road, gasping from the intensity of it. He had to squash this feeling. There was no way that he was jealous about Arnella, no way.

Chapter Two

Arnella woke up with a bitter taste in her mouth. She looked around the guest room where she had been sleeping and grimaced. She couldn't remember how she had gotten there. Was the party even over?

She looked down on herself. She was wearing one of Tracy's nightgowns, a pink fluffy thing that was so Tracy-ish. Pink and girly was Tracy's middle name. She would have preferred to sleep in one of Vanley's old boxers and a ratty t-shirt.

So, what was going on? The last thing she remembered was drinking a drink that David gave her and then feeling dizzy. Cory and Jeff had been around too and they had led her to the poolside changing room.

She raised her head from the pillow when she heard Tracy's mother at the door. She knocked briefly and then stuck her head around it. Her perfectly coifed hair was neat as usual.

"Ah, Arnella," Audrey Carr whispered. "Do you want to

join us for breakfast?"

Mrs. Carr had a soft motherly voice, the type she wished her own mother had. She had always envied Tracy for her mother.

"Breakfast?" she opened her eyes again and looked in Mrs. Carr direction. She was still standing at the door, obviously dressed for work.

"But what about the party? Is it over?"

Mrs. Carr looked as if she nodded. Arnella couldn't be sure because her vision was blurry.

"Tracy said you have been asleep since yesterday afternoon. I was all for calling the doctor when we came in last night and saw that you were still out; I thought it unnatural but Tracy said you were just tired."

Tired? She was not that tired. For the past few days, she had done nothing much except twiddle her thumbs, debating with herself, whether she should call her uncle and throw herself at his mercy. Where did Tracy get her 'tired' story?

"Where's Tracy?" Arnella asked uncomfortably. *What the hell happened to me? Tracy was the only one who would know,* she thought.

"Downstairs," Mrs. Carr said softly. "Your clothes are at the foot of the bed. Please join us; we haven't seen you in quite a while."

Arnella glanced down to the foot of the bed. Her tie and dye, backless, summer dress was there all right. She got up gingerly and wondered why she felt sore all over, even her knees and especially her throat and vagina.

Oh no! I wasn't raped, was I? The thought filled her with dread. At first, her mind wouldn't cooperate with trying to remember, but when she hobbled to the en suite bathroom and stepped under the hot shower, snippets of the previous afternoon came back to her. She remembered Cory behind a video camera, grinning. He was naked.

God, no! please no! Not that nerdy, imbecile who she had rejected time and time again from high school days! But there he was in her mind's eye, naked and grinning. She pushed her mind to remember more but that was all that she saw.

She stepped into the shower and soaped up thoroughly. Out of nowhere came the memory of David, his buzz cut hair in her line of vision as he whispered, "You'll like this, Arnella. All my girlfriends say I am good." Then she remembered him, his face sweaty above her panting, "You are tight, like a virgin," and then she heard chuckles in the background.

Arnella leaned her face down on the tile in the shower cubicle. Was that her giggle she heard in her ears? Was she the one sinuously stretching in front of the camera? Camera! Had they videotaped her in the poolroom? She couldn't be sure if it was a video camera or one that took still images. She wasn't even sure that there had been a camera. Maybe it was the sun coming through the window.

They must have drugged her. The thought gave her goose bumps under the heat of the water. Why would Cory and David do that to her? And Jeff! She remembered his leering face as he rammed his penis down her throat.

A sob threatened to tear from the bowels of her belly, but she managed to swallow it back. She closed her eyes and willed herself to remember the details of what else happened to her, but she couldn't. Her brain felt foggy, and she felt really hung-over, like she had consumed several tons of alcohol, though she could not remember having a drop of alcohol at the party. What could wipe out her memory like this? What had those cretins put in her drink? She had found it strange that all three of them had come to her acting extremely friendly. David had handed her that cup with root beer and had made a quip about success and long life.

She forced herself to get out of the shower. She was not the type to cry about these things, even though she was cringing inside at the thought of them and her together. She closed her eyes, willing the hazy thoughts to go away. She opened her eyes again and stared at the cream finish of the tiles. It was as if her eyes were fixated on the thing. She couldn't make her body move.

She was devastated. She tried to shovel her feeling of being unclean back into that deep vacant hole where all her fears and pain lurked, but it was proving to be quite a task.

She wouldn't show how much this had hurt her. As usual, she would put on her Arnella veneer and act as if it didn't trouble her and move on.

She went back into the shower to give herself a last wash to try to get the unclean feeling to leave her body. She wondered briefly, as she sloughed the water over her head, why it happened to her, as if her life wasn't hard enough as it was.

She quickly finished her shower and pulled on her clothes after she dried herself. The Carr's bathroom was luxurious. They had plush guest towels, perfumes, and all manner of cosmetics to make a person feel special. She rubbed one of the lotions on her skin and thought, *where was Tracy in all of this?* It was her party. Hadn't she suspected what the guys had done?

Arnella swiftly looked in the mirror. She was not one to dwell on her looks, but she checked to see that all her parts were in place. She feverishly scanned her face. She looked fine: no damage to her big brown eyes and arched eyebrows, though her lips looked a little bruised and her nose looked slightly red to her.

She needed to go see a doctor after this and take all the relevant STI tests. She shuddered to think what she might have caught from these guys. She didn't know them that well, nor what their lifestyles were like. She left the room in a hurry, trying to leave her thoughts behind in there as well, and went downstairs to the Carr's vast breakfast room.

Mr. Carr had his head buried in one of the daily newspapers. Tracy was on the phone giggling. She waved to Arnella, and Mrs. Carr was looking at her, concerned.

"Morning all," Arnella said, forcing herself to sound breezy and unaffected.

"Are you feeling all right dear?" Mrs. Carr was sipping her tea and looked at Arnella quizzically, like she wanted to say something more but was feeling her out first.

"Fine," Arnella nodded and sat around the circular table across from Mr. Carr. He was a big man with a huge head and thick curly hair that formed in a peak on his head. He did not have much of a neck, and his extremely light skin had swaths of red all over, like he was permanently flushed. He had two diamond rings on his pinky finger and they twitched when she sat across from him.

Arnella imagined that he was biding his time to address her. He had never liked her, so she would only visit Tracy when he wasn't home. Whenever they happened to meet, he would always have a slight sneer on his lips. Arnella could conclude that he had heard some of the rumors about her and didn't want his precious only daughter to become ensnared with her.

Their helper wheeled in a trolley and started putting items on the middle of the table. She smiled shyly with Arnella, and Arnella grinned back. She had fun times sneaking out of the house through the kitchen in years past when Mr. Carr had arrived home.

The food items included freshly baked bread, and when the scent hit her, Arnella realized how famished she felt. Her belly was rumbling and empty.

Mr. Carr lowered the newspaper. His light skin was freckled, and his left eye was ticking. It was the first time in years that Arnella was actually staring him in the face.

"Are you related to the Bancrofts in the hills?" he asked without preamble.

Arnella nodded slowly, "Yes, why?"

"It says here that Marcus Bancroft has tied the knot with Senator Durkheim's daughter, Deidra, in a surprise twilight ceremony in Kingston. Were you invited?"

Arnella shook her head. "No, I wasn't."

"Oh, so they are distant relatives," Mr. Carr said disappointed. "You know, if I were you, I would claim whatever relation I had with them and attend the university at a reduced cost. I mean, look at you; what do you do?"

"Nothing," Arnella answered him saucily.

She couldn't tell him that her uncle, Ryan Bancroft, president of the university, had insisted, just last year, that she attend the university like her brother Vanley and that he would take care of her fees; neither could she tell him that she is an artist. He wouldn't be interested in that. People like Mr. Carr thought that formal schooling was the only vehicle to success. He reminded her of her uncle in that regard.

"You will amount to nothing, if that's the attitude you have," Mr. Carr raised his eyebrows at her nonchalant attitude. He picked up an English muffin from the pile of food in the middle of the table and then put it back. "How will you feel when all your peers are moving on with their high powered jobs and you are stuck in some dead end job somewhere?"

Mrs. Carr cleared her throat, trying to give her husband the 'cease and desist' look, though she seemed to agree with him.

"What will you do," Mr. Carr was warming up in his diatribe, "when people like my Tracy has to be the one who bails you or your brats out of jail later on in life. Do you want to continue living off your parents?"

Arnella rolled her eyes. "I could always model." She bit into a small cinnamon roll, then grabbed six more and put on her plate; they were good.

Mr. Carr almost snapped. "Do you think that your pretty looks, which you are slowly damaging with all those piercings," he looked at the clip on her nose and the one on her eyebrow, "will last forever?"

Arnella was glad she removed the one on her tongue. She wouldn't put it back on either. She had done it to shock the people around her. Since she had succeeded, she could move on.

"You look ridiculous," he ranted. "As a matter of fact, you look unemployable. Now tell me, which employer in his right mind will want to hire somebody looking like you?"

Arnella continued nibbling her rolls and watched as the vein on the side of Mr. Carr's head got bigger and bigger. "Maybe a mechanic or a construction site wouldn't care much," she said contemplatively, deliberately irking Mr. Carr, who obviously had been building up for years to give her this lecture. His disregard for her was finally finding an outlet.

"I have told Tracy, time and time again, to have nothing to do with you," he raged. His light complexion looked flushed. His neck had bands of dark red across it, despite the central cooling in the house. He looked back at Tracy, who was still on the phone. "I told her to cancel all ties with you. You know why?"

Arnella spooned out some stewed chicken onto her plate and shook her head solemnly. She had some muffin in her mouth so she mumbled a garbled sounding, "no."

"Because you are little more than the scum of society! You contribute nothing! You add nothing! Can you even speak properly?"

Arnella grinned. Obviously, he wanted tears and she was not going to oblige. His wife looked as if she was on the verge of tears on her behalf. The insults were trickling down her back like rain on a smooth surface.

"I would speak, but I have nothing worthwhile to say. At least I don't go around shouting at people I barely know."

"Argh." Mr. Carr growled. "I know you, and I know your type. It's sickening."

"Calm down, dear," Mrs. Carr jumped in quickly to pacify him. She had been listening to her husband berate Arnella, hoping that she could at least be spurred to action, but now she thought her husband had gone too far. He looked as if he was about to jump across the table and choke the life out of Arnella. It didn't help that Arnella was looking at him, unaffected by what he had intended to be a lecture.

Tracy had come off the phone and was looking at her father with a stunned look on her face. "Dad, please," she squealed. "She is our guest. What has she done to you? Why are you attacking her like this?"

"It's not her; it's what she represents," Mr. Carr said with a huff. "She's a worthless piece of trash. Only thing she knows how to do is wear skimpy clothes and sleep around with men for money. I've said it before; I'll say it again. She's a bad influence, Tracy."

Arnella finished off her cinnamon rolls and picked up her orange juice. She might as well have enough to eat and drink now because she was not sure that there was anything in her house.

Her mother had gone to the States for the summer, and her

brother was working at Mount Faith as an intern pastor. The house would be empty; it had been empty of food when she left there for Tracy's party.

Mr. Carr's heated recriminations were not new to her. Since she was a little girl, she had been hearing that she was worthless. She already felt worthless; he was right to a point. So far, she had contributed nothing to society, but she intended to at some point. *What was he contributing?* she thought resentfully. He was a banker. What do they contribute?

She didn't want to go to university to immerse herself in what she considered boring subjects. She didn't want to get a high-powered job like Mr. Carr or Mrs. Carr, who was a dentist, nor did she want to be like Tracy, who was studying to be a lawyer. She wanted to be an artist.

She had several paintings to finish. She just needed the inspiration to finish them, or was it paint she needed? Painting was an expensive mistress. Painting was her dream, but it seemed as if she was a worthless piece of nothing, to hear Mr. Carr tell it.

She got up from the table, her belly full. "I really hope the rant is over because I have to run. Even worthless people have things to do," she said smartly. "Thanks for the breakfast though. You have helped the poor and lowly for the day; that is a great contribution to society. No thanks for the lecture. For a lecture to be effective, the person you are lecturing must be willing to listen to you. I thought your tone was judgmental and self righteous."

"Get out!" Mr. Carr growled. "I don't want to see you around my house again. Make sure she is only taking what she carried." He bellowed as Tracy raced after Arnella.

Arnella hurried through the vast marble-tiled hall to the imposing wood structure with intricate carvings that was the door. Mr. Carr had ordered it from some far away place in the Middle East, and it arrived just last month. As usual, she admired the craftsmanship of the place and the tasteful sculptures dotted around, but she dared not linger.

"Wait, Arnella," Tracy shouted.

Arnella paused with her hands on the door.

"I am sorry about Daddy," Tracy said earnestly. "For the life of me I can't understand why he unloaded on you like that this morning."

"That's okay." Arnella gave her a smile. "I guess I'll not be invited to any cocktail parties hosted by him. By the way, what happened yesterday?"

"What do you mean?" Tracy asked, looking at Arnella wide eyed.

"I woke up in your guest room; obviously something is wrong, I can't remember being there or even spending the night," Arnella whispered, "and I am having little hints of memories. I was having sex with David and Jeff. Please tell me that did not happen; that it was a nightmare."

Tracy frowned. "You disappeared for a while. I was busy with some of my other guests. When I started searching for you, you were fast asleep in the pool room."

"So where were Cory, David, and Jeff?" Arnella insisted.

"I don't know. They must have left. Come to think of it, I never saw them after that."

Arnella huffed, "Those pigs must have drugged me, had sex with me and took off."

"No." Tracy looked surprised. "That can't be. Are you sure you are not hallucinating? You did sleep for most of the evening."

"I am not hallucinating," Arnella said gruffly. "I can't say what really happened but I have little snippets of memory of the three of them doing things to me."

"Then go do a test then and find out what substance is in your body and go do a rape kit too," Tracy said flippantly, pushing her hands in her shorts pockets. "Too bad you bathed this morning, though. That would prove to be a bit of challenge for you to prove anything."

Arnella grunted. "I was violated here. I know I was not dreaming. I woke up with bruises and pain."

She stepped through the door onto the spacious veranda. Tracy walked behind her. "Arnella, I don't want to say you are not thinking straight, but how could that happen to you at my party? David, Cory, and Jeff are old classmates. Come on, you must have been extremely tired. You slept like a log throughout most of the party."

Arnella inhaled angrily; this girl was implying that she did not know what she knew. She clenched her fist and walked down the steps. *Don't get angry* kept ringing in her head. *Don't get angry.* Tracy had managed to do in one sentence what her father with all his bellowing and blustering hadn't done.

She blinked back the tears that were in her eyes and swallowed. She headed to her mother's, half-rusted Volkswagon Bug, which was parked outside of the four-car garage. It looked like it was fit for the junkyard, with its patches of green and blue; one door was yellow. Yesterday when she had driven up to the party, she had tried to park it so that it did not look too conspicuous among the SUV's and the top of the line European cars. Tracy did not have poor friends; she was the only exception, but now she was not too sure she wanted Tracy as a friend anymore. There was something not right about how she was readily supporting Cory, David, and Jeff when she told her about what happened.

"Arnella don't be mad," Tracy said, a pacifying note in her voice, "about what Daddy said in there." Tracy was trying hard to change the subject about Arnella's hallucination.

Arnella decided to bite. She turned around and looked at her, hoping that her face did not display any sort of mistrust. It was hard because she was feeling quite bitter about her lack of support. Arnella was not the type to lie. In fact, she was brutally honest. Why did Tracy so quickly suggest that she was hallucinating?

"Why don't you come and do some art courses at school? I saw an advertisement for an Art certificate," Tracy continued brightly, obviously thinking that Arnella would leave the subject of her party alone. "Mount Faith has a good working student program for those who can't afford it, and I might be living in a studio apartment at Blue Palm next semester, if they accept me. The studio has a living room; you can sleep on my couch till you can afford to pay rent somewhere. I know you aren't closely related to the Bancroft's at Mount Faith, but they are really rich. They should be able to help a poor relative like you."

Arnella opened her mouth to say something about her relatives but quickly closed it with a snap. Why hadn't she ever told Tracy that she was not that distant from the Bancroft's in Mount Faith? It never came up; that's why. Tracy obviously thought she was a charity case. Always had, it seemed.

She did not like the way Tracy mentioned the word 'poor' in her little heart-felt statement just now. The snobbishness was literally dripping from each word. Why hadn't she noticed before how patronizing Tracy was?

She shook her head. "Thanks for the generous offer, Tracy, but I know how to do art. I don't need someone to teach me. I should be teaching it. What I want is a studio, supplies, and time to do my thing. I have to go now." She glanced at her watch, a leather strap timepiece she had taken from her brother. The time had stopped at 2:00 pm. It was malfunctioning like everything else in her life right now. It looked like it was about seven thirty in the morning though.

"If I ever make it up to Mount Faith, it will be because I am too broke and have to throw myself to the mercies of the wealthy Bancroft's. See ya."

"See ya," Tracy said, watching her friend as she yanked open her car door. "By the way, what do you think about Alric?" she asked, anxious to hear Arnella's reply.

"You've have asked me that a million times." Arnella looked back at her, juggling her car keys. "He's okay, in a stuck up sort of way. We have lived on the same street for years. He's a cool dude if you like that type. Your father would have no problem inviting him to supper."

Tracy nodded, satisfied. "Okay then, drive safely."

Arnella waved and got into the car. It took her five tries to start it, all the time wondering if it had something to do with the fact that the fuel gage was on "E". She was going to have to buy gas and then go to a doctor to be checked out. She would prefer to err on the side of caution where the exchange of bodily fluids was concerned. However, that would mean that most of her money would be swallowed up in doctor's bills. She could go to a free clinic instead, but that would take her all day. Then she would head up to Mount Faith to indeed throw herself on the mercies of the wealthy Bancroft's.

Chapter Three

It took Arnella two weeks to make up her mind to go visit her uncle. A girl had her pride, and she was not into begging but her art supplies had run out. She had no money to buy even a small bottle of watercolor paint. Her mother had called the day before saying that she was not sure she would be coming back until November.

Her brother had called to check up on her, and she had tried to sound breezy and light for him, but he had picked up that something was wrong and had begged her to come and stay with him at Mount Faith for the rest of the summer. The summer had two more weeks and then it would be time for the new school term.

Arnella chewed her lip. She might just do that. She had swallowed her pride and asked Vanley for gas money. All she needed now was to grovel at her uncle's feet and find out how he could help her with her art supplies. She hated that she had to ask him, of all the people in the world. He was going to insist that she sign up for some stupid course or do some useless degree.

She thought of her cousin, Micah. He had rebelled but had still done a degree. That was the power of her uncle. She would surely die of boredom if she were to do a degree; all her creativity would dry up, hemmed in by the rigid thoughts of people who couldn't think for themselves. To her, school was a holocaust to creative thinkers.

She sighed and looked around her art room. It was rustic and dramatic. The place had good natural lighting in the day, but the awful artificial lights she had to work with at night didn't lend itself to creating great art. She needed to get proper bulbs for her studio, not the dull ones she now had. She had done a few paintings featuring trees—dying trees. The stark twigs and lifeless brown trunks enhanced the bland beige that she had painted her studio wall. She had completed five paintings, but she wanted to do several more of mostly nature scenes.

She was drawing a scene of driftwood with seaweeds wrapped around it on a beach. She had run out of blue and green. *Driftwood at sunset.* She could already see it in her mind's eye: a lonely scene that seemed peaceful at first glance, but angry waves surrounded it and dark skies blocked the sun. The painting was an allegory of her life.

One by one, she tenderly wrapped her paintings in white sheets and carried them downstairs to her mother's VW bug. At least the car was still holding up. It looked as if it were on its last though. The car was battered and rusting, kind of like her mother's heart, she thought poetically. These days she was thinking poetically a lot. Ever since she got back her STI reports. They were all negative. Thank God. It still didn't negate the fact that she knew something was done to her. She hadn't called Tracy since then, and she was not going to contact her again. It was time to let that particular friendship go. She was never going to be Tracy's sort of people.

She went upstairs for her bag and flung it in the trunk. It had a rusted out circular hole in the bottom, about the size of her fist. She hoped it didn't rain, or her stuff would get wet.

She took one last look around the yard. The grass was overgrown, as usual, and the lone acerola cherry tree that was standing at the front had weeds choking its branches. It looked like something she could paint too, another allegory.

She headed for the door and locked it. It was doubtful that anyone would want to rob the place though. It had nothing of value in it, now that her paintings were gone. She glimpsed, from the corner of her eye in time to see Alric's Audi slowly making its way past the house. She seldom saw him coming around the area anymore, not since Tracy's party. She watched as Alric slowed the car at her gate then wound down his window halfway and looked at her balefully.

What was his problem? She hadn't done anything to him. She headed to her car, ignoring him, but she realized that he had stopped completely. He wound down his window fully and beckoned to her. Arnella was sure that she didn't want to hear what Alric 'holier than thou' Peterson had to say. She was tired of sermons. She got enough from her intern pastor brother, and she was tired of men anyway. Her newest experience with the three rats had cemented that in her mind. She walked to the car door bristling.

"What?" She said hostilely, bending down by the car to look at him fully.

"Good morning to you too, Arnella," Alric said. His voice was well modulated and sounded smooth, like a radio announcer's. *Does everybody who went to that university come out sounding refined?* she wondered.

"Morning," Arnella said. She couldn't keep the abrupt

tone from her voice. Alric had avoided her for the past ten or so years. Why the sudden about face?

"So what grand adventure are you off to?" he asked, gazing at her lazily and then at her opened car trunk.

"Why do you care?" Arnella frowned. "And why are you suddenly talking to me?"

"I thought about it, and I concluded that nobody, not even you, could be as bad as you are made out to be; so I thought I would break the ice, you know, get to know you a bit better like a good neighbor should. I have listened to the gossip about you but realized that I've never once tried talking to you myself."

"Oh, heavens," Arnella sighed, "that sounds like guilty Christian charity talking. When did you decide to do this? You know what I think. I think you shouldn't talk to me in public and in broad daylight. Already, Mrs. Ferguson's curtains are twitching and the Greens and all their children are on the veranda looking over here, wondering if I am going to devour you like a black widow spider. Didn't you hear that I broke up the Spencer's marriage? Slept with old man Spencer, though he is pushing seventy, and caused Mrs. Spencer to have a heart attack?"

"Did you?" Alric asked seriously.

Arnella giggled. He was actually asking her seriously. She didn't bother to answer. "Didn't you hear that I caused the Morison's house to spontaneously combust because I walked past it and pointed over their yard?"

Alric chuckled. "Did you point over there?"

"Of course, I did," Arnella said impatiently, "I was telling their grandchild Jimmy to stop playing with firecrackers on the front lawn. I pointed at the brat threateningly. Told him I was going to call the police. Apparently, somebody saw me wagging my finger and reported that I was casting a spell."

Arnella's belly grumbled. "I have to run, I need food badly."

"You have no food at home?" Alric asked, looking over at the yard, which looked like it needed a gardener, and at the house, which looked like it needed a lick of paint. Alric was sure it wouldn't look so dilapidated if it had both.

"Nope," Arnella said, backing away. "I am one level from begging on the streets."

"Want to come have lunch with me?" Alric asked. "I promised my Mom that I would have lunch with her today. It's her birthday."

Arnella paused. "Your mother, the pastor's wife?"

Alric nodded. "Yes, the pastor's wife. Is that a problem?"

Arnella couldn't think of a thing to say about Mrs. Peterson. She was unfailingly polite and always had a kind word to say. She had dropped her to high school once when she was late and had driven fast to get there because Arnella had been anxious about being late again. "Okay," she said grudgingly, "but only because I am hungry. I hope y'all don't preach at me."

Alric nodded solemnly, looking at her as if she had done him a favor. "I promise, no preaching. Glad to see, though, that the tongue ring and the nose ring are gone." He held up his hand when Arnella frowned. "You'll drive along I presume?"

"Yeah," Arnella nodded, almost jogging to her car. She hoped this lunch would not include chitchatting that would delay partaking of the food.

*****

Arnella drove up to the Peterson's in record time. It was just fourteen houses from hers, at the very end of the cul-de-sac. Her car sputtered as she turned into their curved driveway. It was making a wheezing sound, like it was about to shut off altogether, so she crossed her fingers and hope it would start again when she was ready to leave.

It was the first time she was seeing the house up close. It was obscured from the road with well-placed trees and shrubs. It was on a huge lot, much larger than the lot hers was on. She parked behind Alric's car in the driveway and got out of the vehicle and stretched.

Alric came out of his car and looked her over appreciatively. "You tend to do that a lot, don't you?"

"What?" Arnella asked him curiously then glanced around at the well-maintained grounds.

"Stretch," Alric said. "Three weeks ago, at Tracy's party, you were stretching half naked for everybody to ogle."

Arnella thought of explaining that when she painted she tended to become so immersed in her work that she often forgot to stretch, so she stretched whenever she got the chance, but she didn't say a word. She was okay with Alric thinking whatever he wanted about her.

"About that party," Alric shoved his hand in his pockets.

"Which party?" Arnella rubbed her belly absently.

"The one where you went off with the three guys," Alric said slowly. "I can't believe you did that."

Arnella did not want to talk about that, or even think about it. It was something that she was striving to put behind her. It was three weeks ago and she still had nightmares about it, and she had vowed never again to take a drink from any man in a party setting. She had even considered going to the police but she scrapped that thought. They wouldn't believe her, she was sure, and those guys would just band together and say that she wanted it. That's if they were even willing to admit that they did anything wrong. See, even Alric believed that she went off with them willingly. She shuddered to think about what her reputation was like in his head, if he actually believed that she went with them willingly.

She shrugged. "I can't believe I did it either."

"Does anything get to you?" Alric asked her, genuinely concerned. "Are you really so cold that basic principles and decency escape you?"

The question cut, Arnella admitted to herself, but she had gotten so many cutting blows through the years that she sent it straight to the part of her that processed them but left her shield in place. That's how she coped with insults and even praise; she sent them to a neutral zone in her head.

"Are we going to eat? Or are you going to try to evangelize a hungry person."

Alric sighed. "Come along then."

He headed to the back of the house. They walked on cobblestone around to a shaded patio area. There was a table laid out under a sprawling cashew tree. The atmosphere was cool and tranquil. Arnella felt as if she were in a different world though she lived just up the street. *What a difference money and good taste could make,* she thought.

Mrs. Peterson was sitting at the table. She stood when she saw Alric and Arnella.

"Ah, Alric, I see you brought company. Welcome, Arnella. It's good to see you."

Arnella smiled. "Mrs. Peterson, you haven't changed a bit. Still looking as fresh and young as I remember. Happy Birthday."

"Call me, Joy," Mrs. Peterson said. "And thank you. This is a pleasant surprise Alric, where'd you find Arnella?"

"In her front yard," Alric said. "She's hungry, so I invited her to lunch. I hope that's okay."

"That's fine," Joy smiled at Arnella. She noted that Arnella had lost weight and that her usual jewelry statements were missing. As usual, she had her hair in a messy ponytail and was wearing full black.

She long suspected that Arnella needed some support and help. She had attempted, through the years, to speak to her mother, but that had been unfruitful. Her mother, when she was sober, pretended that all was well in her family.

"I hope you are hungry," Joy said, as she called Kadene to set another place for Arnella. Kadene was there for the week to help with spring-cleaning. Kadene came over and quickly set the table.

"I really am." Arnella said nodding. "I feel as if I was on an involuntary fast."

"Why?" Alric asked.

"Broke! I almost went outside and had some grass to eat." Arnella said, ignoring Alric's incredulous look.

She was salivating and her nose, extremely sensitive to food because she hadn't had any in a while, picked up the aroma of chicken soup. She sniffed the air and smiled. In no time, Kadene was wheeling out a food trolley with soup.

Alric stopped in mid-sip to watch her as she practically gulped down the hot soup. Joy nudged him under the table. 'Stop staring,' she seemed to tell him with her eyes. He looked back down at his soup. The next time he held his head up Arnella had finished her soup.

"So what has been happening around here for the week I've been away at Mount Faith?" Alric dragged his eyes from Arnella and asked his mother.

"Cleaning," Joy said. "Even though Mount Faith is cooler in the summer, it was nice to come back here to air out the house and let the walls know they weren't abandoned. I also caught up on my reading. I am happy that I was not assigned any summer classes to teach."

Alric nodded and gestured for Kadene to keep the food

coming. He was glancing at Arnella who seemed as if she would eat the table if given half a chance.

"I forgot that you teach at Mount Faith," Arnella said after polishing off her last bite of bread. "So Pastor Peterson is the chaplain there, and you go there as well?" she said to Alric. "I bet you all live on the picture perfect Mount Faith Drive too."

Alric nodded. "As a matter of fact we do. It's a recent development though. My parents used to commute. Mommy didn't want to leave the house unoccupied but she finally decided to move when a house became available up there."

Joy laughed. "Coping with the workload is much easier when you live near the campus, and the nursing department, where I teach, is close to Mount Faith Drive. Most mornings I walk to work."

"And for the record," Alric said to Arnella, playfully, "I don't live with my parents. I live at Blue Palm Apartments."

Arnella nodded. "Impressive. I heard there was a waiting list to live there and that you had to be recommended. Tracy was dying to live there last year but they don't allow freshmen."

Alric smirked. "Yes, they have that rule. I waited for two years before I could live there. This will be my final year of Med School so I was given a place on the Nominating Committee; I just might recommend her."

"Sounds good," Arnella said watching as Kadene wheeled platters of food to the table. "Tracy likes you. Living in the same complex will be great for the two of you to get to know each other."

Alric half-smiled. He was sure that she barely heard a word of what he said. She was watching the food trolley with intensity, almost licking her lips in anticipation.

He wondered again how Arnella, who was related to

President Bancroft, could be so different. The Bancrofts were not poor people. Why did she seem so hungry now and drive that battered old car and live in that ugly old house, even though it was in a nice neighborhood.

"Why are you so hungry that you wanted to eat grass?" He blurted out before he could stop it. He had reasoned with himself two weeks ago that he was going to befriend Arnella, not alienate her.

He thought about her far too much for it to be healthy, whether the thoughts were negative or positive. The best thing for him to do was to get to know the woman behind the myth.

"I told you I'm broke. B-R-O-K-E," Arnella said in that deadpan way of hers, spelling the word while she served herself some food. The food was more than enough for three people, so she had no qualms about taking three pieces of chicken. "So my next adventure," she bit into the chicken, "is to go up to Mount Faith to throw my self on my rich relatives and beg them to give me alms." She shoved a forkful of food into her mouth and moaned, "This is good. Whoever cooked this is a gem."

"Thank you, Arnella." Joy grinned. She had deliberately kept silent, watching the byplay between Alric and Arnella. Her son was looking at Arnella as if she was a different specie.

She was terribly frank without guile or subterfuge. What you saw with Arnella was what you got. Joy found it oddly refreshing in a person. There was no guessing with this girl. She was as honest any person as you could find. Either that or she didn't care what others thought of her once she spoke. Obviously, Alric found it rather jarring.

"So why don't you get a job?" Alric asked her, picking up his fork in a far more leisurely manner than she had.

"I have a job," Arnella said mid-chew. "I am a starving artist. I need supplies so I need to beg. When I sell some of my paintings, I'll be fine again. Don't worry about me, grandpa," she said, mocking Alric. "I'll be just fine. I always land on my feet."

Joy laughed out loud, "Grandpa." She wiped her eyes and nodded, pleased. "I think this is one of the most entertaining lunches I have had in recent memory."

Alric just frowned and looked at Arnella. "You are an enigma."

Arnella shoveled more food into her mouth and shrugged, "And you are too much into dogma."

"Do you know what enigma means?" Alric had not even touched his food.

Arnella speared a cooked carrot with her fork and chewed it slowly. "Enigma: a person or thing that is mysterious or hard to understand."

"So you do know." Alric looked at her, a light of understanding in his eyes. "You are not slow-witted are you? You know, I thought you were when you were little. I thought you were a feral child; you would look at people and growl and curse those filthy bad words. I thought the tons of weed that I heard you smoked was responsible for that. I heard that you used to go to the bush and chain light cigarette after cigarette that was filled with marijuana that you had personally planted."

Arnella put down her fork and giggled. "How old was I when I did this?"

"Ten," Alric said. "That's what everybody in the neighborhood said about you."

"And I told him not to listen to gossip," Joy interjected.

Arnella picked up her fork again. "I am not slow witted when I eat." She cleared her plate. "Are you going to eat, or are you going to try to solve the mystery of Arnella?"

"Eat," Alric said, scooping up a forkful, "I have a feeling the mystery of Arnella would take years to solve if the mystery can even be solved."

Arnella snickered. "I have heard that rumor before: that I smoked tons of weed. It's fascinating though. My neighbor to the left, Tommy Turner, must have come up with that one. I caught him smoking weed, so of course I told him I was going to tell his mother. He told on me first and what a whopper it was."

Alric raised his eyebrows. "Really?"

"Really," Arnella giggled. "Cross my heart. I have never tried to smoke, or drink. I am a clean living girl. Vanley would kill me if he found out I was anything other than upstanding."

Joy chimed into the conversation. "You know, Alric, I have never believed a word I've heard about Arnella."

"Not even the story about how she ran away from home when she was fourteen," Alric said, "and lived with a Catholic priest as his girlfriend?"

Arnella laughed. "You sound so offended."

Alric shook his head. "Not offended, disgusted! Disgusted at the priest for having a girlfriend and at you for being his girlfriend. You were underage!"

Joy interrupted her son, "Arnella, I heard that your cousin Marcus got married. That's nice."

"I heard so too," Arnella nodded. "It was a quick thing. Only close relatives were asked to attend. Deidra did not want to have a circus for a wedding, with a million and one of her father's political buddies, so she kept it to just immediate family and their closest friends, especially because Marcus is a celebrity. Kylie said it was really romantic. She keeps me in touch with all the family news."

"I saw Adrian the other day; his wife had a son," Joy said, steering the conversation from Arnella's supposed wicked ways, but Alric was itching to take it back up.

Arnella nodded. "Yes, Cathy had a boy. He is super cute. Looks just like Avia, their daughter. I really like Cathy."

"You would," Alric snorted. "Wasn't she an exotic dancer or something? Sounds like something you'd do."

"I can't dance around a pole to save my life. I think it has something to do with my lack of coordination. I've tried it though." She winked at him suggestively and then laughed when he grimaced. "I like Cathy because she is a genuinely nice person. Last Christmas, when I stayed with my uncle, I spent a lot of time with her."

Joy turned the topic to other neutral things while Alric studied Arnella. He drank in her features; he didn't care if his mother saw how intently he was doing it.

Without her heavy mascara on, he could see that she had natural eyelashes that were so thick that they looked like they were clumped together. They shielded big brown eyes that were the deepest brown, almost black. She had a straight little nose and a generous mouth, which was brushed with the faintest pink. Her skin was light and blemish free, except for a birthmark on her lower right shoulder. He remembered seeing it at the pool party.

Why he remembered that in such stark detail after all this time was a strike against him, he berated himself. He preferred higher standards in a woman, and Arnella was obviously free with her favors and didn't care who knew it. He still gritted his teeth when he thought of that guy, David, with his hand on her buttock, cupping it in an intimate way. He had seen him around campus this summer. He had been doing summer classes. They were all in the same faculty of science. He had been tempted, several times, to ask them where they had disappeared to with Arnella but had decided against doing so.

"I have to go now." Arnella stood up after they had sung happy birthday to Joy and had a slice of cake. She got another slice to take with her on her journey as well. "Thank you so much for lunch. You may have saved my life."

"So, who are you going to stay with at Mount Faith?" Alric asked, standing as Arnella made to leave.

Arnella shrugged. "I have no idea. I could stay with my brother or my uncle or my cousin Micah. His house is finished and it looks gorgeous; he has room. I saw it in December. He is the most laid back of my cousins—should be fun to stay with him."

Alric wanted to prolong his conversation with her, and he didn't know why. They had reached the front of the house, and the question that was eating away at him like termites in wood popped out involuntarily. "So how was it with three guys? Is it something you do regularly?"

Arnella stopped abruptly and spun around to him. "I don't want to talk about that ever. You hear me? Stop bringing it up! What's it to you anyway?"

"I have never met a more morally bankrupt person in my life," Alric said simply, "you are like fire, dangerous and beautiful. You can't help but stare at it but you know you should keep far from it because you can get burnt."

Arnella hissed her teeth. "Then don't get burnt, Alric. Tracy is a lovely rich girl who is not morally bankrupt. Be fascinated with her. She likes you."

She walked to her car and got in jerkily. She had to slam the door twice for it to close. She hung her head outside the front window, and said, "See you around," then drove away.

Alric stood in the driveway inhaling her car's exhaust fumes and wishing that his fascination with her wasn't burning brighter than ever.

Chapter Four

Arnella paced outside the president's building for what felt like hours. She had finally arrived at Mount Faith, but she didn't want to face her uncle. He was particularly stern with her because in December, when she spent the Christmas with them, he had strongly encouraged her to come up to Mount Faith for school.

After Kylie's wedding, she had sneaked out of the house and went back to Santa Cruz without telling him goodbye. She just could not take the constant nagging about her lifestyle, but now she was desperate.

She glanced at her watch; it was three o' clock. If she didn't stop the pacing, she would make herself hungry. She slowed down, took a deep breath, and walked into the building. Better face the music now while she still had the strength.

The receptionist looked up at her enquiringly when she leaned on the desk.

"Is Doctor Bancroft in?" she asked, hoping perversely, that

the receptionist would say "no". That way, she could say that she had tried to see him but it hadn't worked out.

"He is in," the receptionist said, "but he won't be for long. He is heading out for a meeting shortly."

"Okay," Arnella heaved a sigh. "Could you tell him Arnella is here to see him?"

"Yes," the receptionist nodded. She spoke briefly on the phone and hanged up. "His office is the last door down the hallway."

Arnella sighed again and headed to the office. She had been to the office before and didn't need the receptionist to tell her where it was. She had just been stalling for time.

She opened the imposing door and stepped into the plush interior. The decor was changed to red and gold. It was beautiful. The red was bold and warm and somehow tamed by the gold. She stood at the door and Ryan Bancroft coughed.

"Ehem, the run away niece," Dr. Bancroft said, removing his reading glasses and folding his arms over a swathe of papers.

"The stating of the obvious uncle," Arnella said fearlessly, going further into the room and sitting before his desk.

"You are here in my office, my territory," Dr. Bancroft said a hint of pleasure in his voice, "so you must want something."

Arnella nodded, "I do."

"You look slimmer," Ryan said, "too slim. Like you've been starving yourself or are you trying to get into the modeling world?"

Arnella shrugged. "I heard that you can't be too rich or too thin, and I am too short to model."

Bancroft chuckled, "I see you have come with your acerbic wit. You are not playing the humble card even though you want something?"

"No," Arnella said, "I don't think people should play around with humility, it's either you are, or you are not. You and I are not humble people."

Bancroft nodded. "Good point. So tell me; what do you want?"

"Money," Arnella said, "for art supplies and a place to crash for a while until I can get my paintings done."

Bancroft started shaking his head. "No!"

"Why not?" Arnella asked, a touch desperately. He had never told her "no" before. He had always tried to help her and Vanley because their father had died when they were little, and he had felt responsible for them. He had been their sole provider for years, until he found out that their mother was drinking away the money he sent to them for food.

"Because," Bancroft got up and reached for his jacket that was on a stand, "you need to do something for me. The money will have to come with strings attached."

"What?" Arnella growled. "I hope it's nothing illegal."

"It is not illegal, on this side of the world, for women to attend university. So no, it is not illegal." Bancroft sneered. "You are going to do an associate degree in general studies for two years. That's all I ask."

"That's unfair!" Arnella shouted. "Why can't you just accept that I don't want to go to school? High school was enough. I passed all my subjects with high honors"

"Only because I insisted," Bancroft leaned on the desk, "and let it be known that I was so proud that you finished. I feel I have a responsibility to you, like I do for my own daughters, and it would be grossly unfair if you did not get a chance to do at least an associate degree. The General Studies associate degree here is pretty flexible. You get to do courses in English, mathematics, biology, physics, computer science, history, philosophy, art, and a foreign language.

Maybe you should choose French as your language. The summer Olympics will be in France next year, and Marcus is hoping to participate. You can go support your cousin and get a first hand feel of the language."

Arnella was about to rant, but she loved the sound of going to Europe and learning a new language. Her uncle was dangling that in front of her like a carrot.

"Did you say art?"

"Yes." Bancroft glanced at his watch. "There are some art courses in the general studies line up. I am sure you will shine there, and the best part is that if you ever decide to do your bachelor's degree, I will help you."

"I won't want to," Arnella said sullenly.

"But you'll do this?" Bancroft asked impatiently.

"Yes," Arnella said reluctantly. "The things people have to do for money."

Bancroft chuckled. "Your problem, Arnella, is that you have no concept of what people have resorted to for money, and my hope is that you never will."

Arnella got up, "I am not staying with you and Aunt Celeste for two years."

Bancroft put his hand in the small of her back and they walked to the door.

He turned back, grabbed his checkbook from a drawer, and scribbled on it swiftly. "Here; this is enough money to cover your art supplies and whatever else you may need in the short run. I don't care where you stay, once you take care of yourself properly. I will put an allowance in your account for the first year. The second year you better find yourself a job."

Arnella exhaled and took the check; he was more generous than she expected. Tears crept into her eyes and she batted them back. What was wrong with her? She did not usually cry.

"Thanks, Uncle Ryan."

Bancroft hugged her around the neck and they walked to the door. "Don't you dare stay away so long when you know you need help," he said gruffly. "You are Oswald's only girl. I often wish I had taken you and Vanley from that mother of yours when you were growing up."

He reached the office door. "Stay out of trouble. Classes for the next semester officially start the first week in September, three weeks from now. If you are not there, I am going to hunt you down and drag you here kicking and screaming."

"Yes, Sir." Arnella smiled weakly and headed out of the building, feeling a little brighter than when she arrived.

Next stop would be a house on Mount Faith Drive. She drove slowly toward it.

The house did not have any room that would be conducive to painting, but despite her forced school attendance, she was not going to neglect her first love. What was she going to do?

*****

When she drove up to the house, the gate was open, and a late model Mercedes was in the driveway. Deidra was standing beside it, talking and laughing with Kylie, who had one of those designer puppies under her arms.

"Hey," she waved to them when she got out of the car.

"Hey," both Kylie and Deidra said to her at the same time.

"What are you doing up here?" Kylie asked, hugging her when she came closer to them. "You never told me you were coming, I could have arranged for us to hang out."

"Uncle Ryan demanded that I come to school for two years, so we'll have all the time in the world to hang out." Arnella sniffed. "What are you two doing here, especially you, the new Mrs. Bancroft?"

Deidra grinned. "I love hearing that. I came for some stuff from my house and Kylie was here so I stopped by. So, are you going to live here now?" Deidra asked, looking at her bags in the back of the car.

"Not sure," Arnella shook her head, "I won't have anywhere to paint if I live here. All the rooms are too small and doesn't have enough light for my purposes."

"You paint?" Deidra asked surprised. "What do you paint?"

"Anything that catches my eye," Arnella shrugged. "The other day I started sketching handbags, of all things; I have a whole folder with them."

"Handbags?" Deidra's eyebrows rose. "That's my sort of business. Let me see what you have."

Arnella shook her head. "I don't want to..."

"Show her," Kylie interjected before she could finish her protest. "I have seen your work before and you are really good."

Arnella sighed and reached into the back of the car for one of her sketchbooks. She handed it to Deidra and turned her back dramatically. She usually felt odd when people were looking at her work in front of her.

"Only handbags are in that book." She looked over her shoulder as Deidra scanned through the sketchbook. "You can tell me if you hate them you know; I won't mind."

"I can't believe it." Deidra had spread the sketchbook on the trunk of her car and was leafing through. "You designed these from out of your head?"

"Yes." Arnella spun around reluctantly.

Deidra pointed at one picture. "This would look good in a soft brown leather. This," she pointed to the opposite page, "would look positively divine in black and white."

She turned the pages slowly and then looked up at Arnella. "You are a genius. Such detail. Such design. You could rival any fashion house with these. I could come up with some shoes to match these. Hunter green, suede, leather."

"So you like them?" Arnella asked slowly.

Deidra shook her head, "No, girl. Like is too mild a word. I love them. Here's the thing. I can sell them for you. Share the profit fifty-fifty."

"Are you serious?" Arnella asked Deidra, who was looking excited enough to burst.

"I have been waiting for some unique way to take the market by the storm and here, you just gave me the idea," Deidra said, her head filling with styles and designs to go with the handbags. "I am going to call these Nella—Nella handbags, and Dee Bee shoes. Oh, Arnella, you are a Godsend. I have some shoe ideas that would be perfect with these bags."

Arnella grinned. "Thanks."

"No." Deidra was happily packing up the sketchbook. "Thank you. You know, if you really want a place to stay, I have a house further up in the hills. The basement is south facing with lots of natural light. You can paint to your hearts content. My sister Charlene won't mind the company. Just yesterday she called me complaining that she's lonely alone in the house."

"But Char will soon marry Micah, so Arnella may have the house all to herself soon," Kylie said cheerfully.

"And," Deidra pulled out her car keys from her bag, "here are the keys to my brother James' old car. It's in the garage doing nothing. I was going to have my father sell it, but here you are. Maybe you should park that in a junkyard somewhere." She looked at Arnella's mother's car and turned up her nose.

"You are a snob," Kylie said, laughing. "I think Arnella's car is classically rustic."

"No," Deidra said, "sorry Arnella, you are about to become

a brand, and brand people don't drive around in rust buckets. Nella bags. I can't wait. So, I'll send you the contract for these designs. As soon as they start selling, you'll start getting paid. In the meantime, sketch fashion to your hearts content and call me when you have a lot."

Arnella nodded, gripping the new car keys in her hand and feeling a little surreal. She didn't even know what type of car it was; all she knew was that it had to be much better than the one she was currently driving.

"Oh, I need your number," Deidra said excitedly. "We can talk periodically. Kylie will show you where the house is, and Char will give you a set of keys. I'll call her later and let her know she is going to have company."

Just like that, Arnella had gone from starving artist, to a university student and a handbag designer with a studio in the hills.

Chapter Five

Arnella walked around in the house she shared with Charlene. She still couldn't believe that she was living there. Everything was just so expensive-looking and clean. It was her second day there after her encounter with Deidra, and her head was still spinning at the swiftness with which her circumstances had changed. If she had known that this was how things would turn out, she should have packed up her stuff and moved to Mount Faith a long time ago, but all things happen in their own time.

The basement that Deidra recommended was huge, airy, and well lit. It was just right for her needs. Charlene had helped her clean up a shelf in her greenhouse for her to store her paints when she buys them. All she needed now were several more easels and she would look like an honest to goodness painter.

She was living her dream, except for that promise she made to her uncle that she would be attending the university for two years, pursuing General Studies. It sounded like hell to her.

She sat in one of the overstuffed chairs in the living room and stretched and rubbed her neck. She had a shiny clean black Honda to drive, and she lived in a mansion. Surely, something bad was going to happen to her.

Nothing good ever happened to her without something terrible happening after. She remembered when she lived in West Virginia with her dad, mom, and big brother. She had been happy; life was cozy; she was loved. Suddenly, when she was eight, a stern-faced policeman had come to the door and told her mother that her father was dead—killed in a bar room brawl.

For years, she thought that bar room brawl story had been a lie. In her recollection, her father had not shown any signs of being an alcoholic. How could he be in a bar, involved in a brawl?

Her mother had broken down after her father died. She changed from the happy, well-adjusted housewife and mother to a vacant-eyed alcoholic. The transition happened in less than a year.

Her Jamaican grandmother had died and left a house and some money in a will. Her mother had packed them up and moved to what Arnella saw as a strange country with strange people, tearing her from her friends and all she held dear.

Vanley, who was six years older, had held her in the nights when she cried herself to sleep because her mother had not quit drinking when she returned to Jamaica. Instead, she had gotten worse. That was when Arnella had taken on her tough exterior. She had turned into a little horror. Her brother had started boarding school shortly after coming to Jamaica, so he had no idea of how bad Arnella had it at home with a bitter woman who thought that her world had collapsed around her.

Arnella had taken solace in painting. She had always received art supplies from her uncle Ryan, who had taken a very keen interest in them after his brother died. Arnella had also taken to running away, sometimes running to strangers, especially when her mother got so drunk that she would beat her for nothing at all.

Things had gotten so bad at home that one day she had stowed away in the local Catholic priest's car. Father Michael had been on his way to Kingston, and when he found her, he had taken her to an orphanage in downtown Kingston that was run by nuns. She had been missing for two weeks before the nuns realized that the Arnella Bancroft being featured on television and Nella Parks, the name she had given them, were one and the same person. She hadn't wanted to leave the orphanage. Three square meals a day without the drunken attacks from her mother had been heaven.

Incidentally, that had been the turning point in her mother's addiction. Her Uncle Ryan had stepped in and gotten her into rehab. By then, Arnella was as hard as a turtle's shell. She had become cynical and bitter, believing that nothing good ever happened to her without a crushing bad following.

She bit her lip when flashbacks of her most recent incident with the guys resurfaced in her mind. She needed to confront them about it. Why had they done that to her? She got up from the overstuffed chair and started pacing again. She had thought that those memories of them violating her would eventually go away, just like her other bad experiences, but they always seemed to resurface. She kept remembering the afternoon with a hazy cloud surrounding it. She couldn't recall specifics, and the not knowing spooked her even more.

Her first recall was David panting on top of her. Then there was Jeff assaulting her orally, and Cory... She couldn't remember what he did. She only recalled his grinning face operating a camera or had he been standing in the light?

She should report it, but a part of her was reluctant. She hated when people disbelieved her—she hated that with a passion. Who would believe her anyway? Even Alric thought that she had gone off with them, and Tracy thought she was hallucinating, and from her fuzzy recall of the events, she hadn't been exactly comatosed in her reactions.

She ran her fingers through her hair and pulled it slightly.

"Hey, Nella."

"Hey, Micah." She gulped in a deep breath. This thing was haunting her. She injected some enthusiasm into her voice.

When she looked up, Micah was standing in the doorway with Taj, her other cousin. In her head, she called him Uncle Ryan's indiscretion. When she had heard the story, she had found it funny. Uncle Ryan was always pretending that he was above reproach. Taj was proof positive that he was not.

"Hi," Taj said to her. He came further into the room. "Micah said you needed easels."

"Oh," Arnella hit her forehead, "I just mentioned it in passing to Charlene. I have a whole lot of space down in the basement that I could put easels. What are you guys here for?"

Taj looked at Micah. "To help you move in. Micah said we should be building easels for you. I am itching to get my hands dirty."

"That's right." Arnella nodded. "You are a psychiatrist. Not much dirtiness with that job. Well, I could do with six easels. It's pretty simple to do." She got up. "Want me to show you guys what I want?"

They followed her down a shallow flight of stairs into the vast the basement. She had thrown white sheets on most of her paintings except one: the seascape with the driftwood.

"That's lovely," Taj said, going closer to it. "You are talented; granted, I am no art appraiser, but this looks really good."

"It's not done," Arnella said shyly.

Taj moved away from the art and examined it, rubbing his chin. "The piece has a quality of loneliness, even despair to it...quite moving."

Arnella gasped; how on earth did he discern that from the piece? Those were her emotions most of the time. Taj looked at her while Micah went toward the easels, examining them and making grunting noises. "You can come see me," Taj said softly. "My services are free for students, even more so for cousins who I know nothing much about."

Arnella swallowed. She wanted to laugh off his offer, but her voice sounded hoarse, and weak instead of mocking and detached. "I don't need a psychiatrist."

"No, you don't," Taj said, nodding, "but I sense that you need to talk. It's my job to listen."

"I talk through my art," Arnella said. "That's my therapy."

After Arnella showed them out, and she and Charlene were left chitchatting in the living room. She remembered Taj's offer and tried to bury it. She didn't need a psychiatrist, whether they were free or family; she was fine. It took her the best part of the night repeating that mantra before she finally accepted it.

*****

Tracy called Arnella on a whim. She hadn't heard from her since her father had given her that upbraiding at the house. She wanted Arnella to know that she was moving into her new place at Blue Palm Apartments and that she was going to start classes tomorrow. She hoped the news would somehow affect Arnella, maybe make her jealous.

The truth is, she had listened to her fathers rant on Arnella and had loved every word. She had only pretended to be on the phone, but she really wanted Arnella to suffer a little because nothing ever really affected her. She had watched and waited for Arnella to break down, especially when her father had called her trash, but Arnella had calmly kept on eating while the words rolled off her easily.

What would it take for Arnella to feel something? There had to be something that mattered to her. She needed to be taken down a peg or two. Surely, she was not immune to the lesser emotions of humanity like fear, sorrow, and confusion. Arnella had always been invincible against hard knocks. The girl was solid as a rock. She shrugged through tragedy and laughed through pain. It had always been a source of envy for Tracy, who thought at the back of her mind that Arnella was a robot.

Nothing touched her in high school. Tracy used to study her and tried to act like her because the more nonchalant Arnella behaved the more people flocked to her. Tracy had had to work for every single friendship she had, not so for Arnella. During high school, some girls had once teased her that she had all the money and Arnella had all the looks and personality.

Tracy had always remembered that, and resented it. She had a love/hate relationship with Arnella. She had deliberately invited Arnella to the party so that she could see that she had many other friends, most of whom were more mature friends and university students.

She had wanted to highlight the differences between them and watch while Arnella displayed some type of jealousy, but she hadn't. She had acted the way she had always acted. To make matters works, even weeks after the party, some of her mature university friends were still asking about Arnella.

That was the reason she liked Alric Peterson so much: he disliked Arnella. At first, she had dragged Arnella to meet him at the university church just to test to see if he would like her. She gave all men, the 'Arnella test' before she dated them. If they liked Arnella, that was it. She would lose all interest in them, but when she had introduced Alric to Arnella, he had looked shocked and dismayed.

That had been a good sign. Arnella was in a maroon red dress that fit her beautifully; even a jealous Tracy could see that. However, Alric had told her, quietly, that he already knew Arnella and asked if she was sure she wanted Arnella for a friend. No, she didn't want her for a friend. Tracy had thought gleefully but she served her purposes. The question had been music to her ears. Usually when she introduced any boy to Arnella, they seemed more interested in Arnella. Conversations usually descended into an Arnella lovefest.

Arnella was fun and unconventional. Arnella was witty and daring. *Arnella needed to be cut down a size or two,* Tracy thought resentfully, but how do you hurt a dog that was already down and was not even whimpering?

Well, she could always brag a little and throw in some concern for her well-being while she highlighted how great her life was turning out. With that in mind, she dialed Arnella's number, picturing her in that dingy old house where she lived, having nothing to do and having no company except her rusty old car, and her little paintings which were not that good in her opinion.

"Hey, Nella," she said sweetly when Arnella answered the phone. "I haven't heard from you for all of three weeks. What have you been doing with yourself?"

"Hey, Tracy," Arnella sounded happy. Tracy sat up straighter in her settee and pressed the phone closer to her ear. Why was she so happy?

"How's it going?" Tracy asked, willing her voice to have an even tone.

"Well," Arnella said slowly, "I am at Mount Faith. My uncle convinced me to stick around, and I am going to be doing two years of school: an associate degree in General Studies. Can you believe it? Tomorrow I have, of all things, Biology and then Bio lab, and Music Appreciation. I appreciate music; why do I need that class? I tell you."

Tracy felt her skin grow hotter and hotter in anger. Who was Arnella's uncle? She didn't know Arnella had an uncle.

"You are up here? Great. I was calling you to tell you that I had settled into my new apartment, and that I was gearing up for my second year of pre-law."

"Good for you. All the best in your school year," Arnella said.

"So where are you staying?" Tracy asked. She couldn't believe that Arnella was actually in university. Who was paying her fees? Mount Faith was one of the most expensive universities in the country. She had had doubts that Arnella was even related to the Bancrofts at Mount Faith. Now she was not so sure.

Arnella was going to be the center of attention soon, she could bet. Why did her father have to give her that speech about college? She had enjoyed being the friend who was going to college. She had enjoyed rubbing it in. She had liked the idea of Arnella being the underdog and she being the benevolent friend. With Arnella coming to the school, that would change in a moment.

"I am staying in a house called Buena Vista," Arnella laughed. "I have never in my life stayed in a place that had its own name. It's gorgeous up here."

"Where is that?" Tracy felt a tight hand squeeze her chest

in jealousy.

"In the hills. Not too far from school," Arnella said breezily. "Tell you what, I'll invite you to lunch. I'll cook. Charlene's been teaching me to do a few basic dishes."

Who is Charlene? Tracy asked in her head, but she didn't want to ask out loud. All the wind was officially taken out of her sail. "Okay, sounds fun," she answered Arnella, and then in a completely fake happy voice asked, "Wouldn't it be great if we had classes together. I mean, if you are doing general studies, we are bound to meet up sometime."

"It would be okay," Arnella said, her voice becoming lackluster, "I am not getting excited about any of these classes. Got to go, Charlene is calling me."

Who is Charlene? Tracy asked to the dead phone. She flung it down on the floor. So, Arnella was already up here and making friends? She wondered how close Arnella was to the Bancroft's up here. She had always referred to them as her rich relatives, but somehow, she had always thought she meant it in a vague way.

She gritted her teeth and looked in the mirror. She had a definite muffin top in her jeans. She had indulged a little bit too much over the summer. She was ordinary looking, she bemoaned. If only she weren't, then she wouldn't envy Arnella so much. As they grew older, that was one of the reasons she had stopped being close to Arnella. The girl showed her up.

Tracy looked at her profile in the mirror. She had long, almost waist length hair, which was thick like a rope. Her skin was light brown; her eyes were pale brown; her nose was a little puggish, and her mouth a bit wide. When you put her features together she was not pretty; she was fairly ordinary in her eyes. She didn't pass muster, especially when standing beside the petite Arnella. Drat it, why was Arnella up here? This was her territory.

Chapter Six

Arnella walked into her Biology lab reluctantly. There was a smaller group of students in the lab compared to the larger Biology class. She had opted for the morning lab because she needed to leave the evenings free to do her painting.

The instant she entered the lab she spotted David Hudson, the guy who had drugged her and raped her, sitting without a care in the world. She went to the back of the lab and sat on one of the wooden stools, but her mind would not settle. She drummed her finger on the table.

David looked back at her, waving nervously.

Did he seriously think that I was going to wave back and pretend like everything was splendid? He had a next think coming, the louse. She glanced at her watch. She had ten minutes until class began. She got up and advanced toward him.

David spun around and swallowed nervously when he saw her approaching. "I didn't know you were coming to college,

Nella," he said pleasantly.

The girls on both side of him looked at her curiously.

Arnella gritted her teeth. "You pig. You nasty, slimy pig."

"Keep your voice down," David said grinning, but behind the grin was a sense of fear. Arnella could sense the fear, and it made her even angrier. She jumped on him and wrapped her hands around his throat.

David started fighting for breath. "Get her off of me."

Arnella held on to his neck for dear life. She was going to kill him right there in class. She applied more pressure to his neck and dug her fingers even more deeply. She saw his twisting face, his eyes growing larger as he struggled for breath, and she imagined that these same eyes were above her violating her. She squeezed his neck harder.

"Stop it, Arnella!" Alric's voice got through the pain and anger that held her in its grip, and she slowly released David, who was coughing and wheezing. The rest of the class, all fifteen students were standing around looking on in varying degrees of shock.

"You are crazy," David gasped out, backing away from her as she made to go toward him again.

Alric held her arm and dragged her outside.

"You should have let me kill him," Arnella said, shrugging from his grip. Tears were in her eyes and coursing down her cheeks. She wiped away the tears impatiently. "I would have done it, you know."

"I can't have you doing that," Alric said calmly. He watched as her breathing returned to normal and said wryly, "What did he do to you to make you so angry?"

Arnella shook her head. "I don't want to say."

Alric sighed. "I hate to come between a lover's tiff."

Arnella, who had turned her head from Alric, not wanting him to see her cry, spun around and looked at him viciously.

"We are not lovers."

Alric held up his hand. "Okay. Sorry. It just seemed like it. Are you attending the school now?"

"Yes," Arnella said, rubbing her hands together and then stretching them. "I am doing General Studies."

Alric nodded. "Your uncle insisted, huh?"

"Something like that." Arnella inhaled deeply.

"And you are doing biology lab?" Alric asked, looking at her. She was in a deep green long sleeved top that molded to her curves, and black pants with green pinstripes. Ordinary wear, but on her it looked special. He hoped she'd say no to the lab because he was the lab instructor and she was a distraction.

"Yes," Arnella said wearily, "but I can't do lab with him in there. I would probably find some way to poison him or burn him with fire or whatever you science types do with lab equipment and chemicals."

She looked behind Alric and into the classroom. David was still having trouble breathing. The two girls who sat beside him were trying to comfort him.

"Okay," Alric sighed, "I am your lab teacher; I am going to have to ask one of you to leave class if that's the way you feel about him."

Arnella winced. She wasn't going to be in the same class with David, and if she did not go to labs, which was 40% of her overall grade, she would probably fail. "I can't do the lab in the evening; I have work to do."

Alric frowned and looked from her to David. "Okay then, I'll ask him to leave."

Arnella nodded. "Thanks Alric. I thought I would be the one you kicked out."

"Don't mention it. Welcome to Mount Faith by the way, and I am not sure that I would ever kick you out."

He went inside and spoke to David. He nodded and got up. He walked through the classroom door slowly and glanced at Arnella, who was standing at the door. He cautiously pushed the door and came through, keeping his back close to it and creating as much spare inches between them as he could manage.

"Look, Arnella," he wheezed as he slowly shuffled along the wall, "I am sorry okay. It was a stupid thing to do, what we did."

"Was there a tape, a video or something?" Arnella hissed, glancing at the class behind her who were trying to hear what was being said.

"We destroyed it," David said. "Honest we did. We realized that it was wrong. You were just lying there like a rag doll passed out cold after a while and we got scared. Cory thought you were dead, and he removed the SD card from the video camera and threw it in a bin."

"Why did you do it?" Arnella asked. "Why me? I thought we were good from high school?"

"We had a little too much to drink and we sort of dared each other." David coughed.

"So you drugged me?" Arnella asked incredulously, "and had sex with me?"

"It was Cory's idea to drug you." David inched passed her. "Blame him. He set up everything."

"You were the one who had sex with me," Arnella said, "the rest didn't. At least I don't remember. You know what I think. I think it was your idea. You stupid cow! I am telling you now…sleep with one eye open, look over your shoulder. I am going to get you."

David actually looked afraid after her vicious reply.

Arnella made to go inside the classroom and then spun around and kicked him in his balls. The last she saw of him was that he was hunched over near the steps. *Serves him right,* she thought angrily.

After the class, Arnella was slowly packing her books into her bag. The guys in the class had given her a wide berth and the girls were treating her as if she was a leper. It didn't bother her in the least. She was used to people treating her as if she had some kind of disease.

Alric had kept glancing at her during the class, probably waiting for her to explode. He was standing at the front of the class now, glancing through the completed activity papers with one hand in his lab coat. He looked so professional standing there, and it had been a good class, well, the parts she allowed her mind to absorb. He would make a good teacher if he weren't planning to be a doctor.

She guessed he had another lab class to teach because he was not shifting from where he stood at the front. She had wanted a quiet time alone to ponder what David had told her. She guessed that she would have to go to the Student Lounge. She had Music Appreciation in two hours. She got up from her chair. It made a scraping sound on the floor. Alric looked up and opened his mouth to say something; he changed his mind and looked back down at the papers in front of him. He was trying to ignore her, she guessed. She didn't care much. She walked past him and headed to the door.

"Why'd you attack him?" he asked her before her hand could reach the door handle.

She bit back an angry retort and then swallowed. Alric at least deserved some explanation; he was allowing her to do morning labs and had kicked David out of the class.

"He did something terrible to me. That was a small taste of what he can expect if he sees me again." She would have loved to tell him the truth, but she was not the type to go around complaining about her life. Besides, Alric would not believe her if she told him the whole story. He saw her as some kind of femme fatale who had no self-control. How had he put it? "She had no moral principles."

She looked at Alric. Her eyes were dry and flat. "You should have let me kill him."

Alric grinned. "No. That would be the ultimate. You know out of all the rumors I have heard about you, murder has not featured in any of them. I have another lab in an hour. Want to hang out here for a while?"

Arnella shrugged and turned back, putting her knapsack down on the table closest to her and sat down on one of the chairs. She put her head on her hands and looked at Alric lazily.

"I didn't know you taught classes here."

Alric nodded. "It was a favor for a friend of mine. I did it for the summer, and I will continue for this semester. It will look good on my resume when I apply for the teaching hospital here. They consider everything."

"Good for you. Sounds fascinating." She looked down on her nails. There was a little hangnail on her pinky, that she was itching to bite off. She resisted the urge and looked back up at Alric who was watching her intently.

"Chewed up nails is a sign of nervousness," he said, pointing to her battered nail pads.

"I am not nervous," Arnella said, though she was feeling a little jittery inside. The feeling had persisted from she saw David in class today. Her body had not lost that feeling, even after an hour.

Alric leaned back in his chair. "Can we play twenty questions?"

"No. Too childish," Arnella said, lying on her hands. " Besides, I don't want to know anything about you."

Alric grinned. "I was thinking of questioning you."

"Okay, shoot," Arnella said. "I do reserve the right to not answer anything I don't want to though."

"Good." Alric rubbed his hands together. "Did you really run away to live with Father Michael?"

"No," Arnella said lazily, "I ran away from home. I had to get out of the house. Father Michael was a convenient escape route. He was at his church and he was packing supplies to go to Kingston. He left all his car doors opened and I was passing by so I went along for the ride."

Alric shook his head. "So where'd you go?"

"Lived with nuns in a children's place of safety in Kingston," Arnella said smiling. "They served rocky road ice cream on Sundays."

Alric frowned. "Why'd you run away?"

"I was unhappy." Arnella closed her eyes.

"Why were you unhappy?" Alric asked softly.

Arnella shrugged. "I am always unhappy. That day I was unhappier than most." She looked at Alric, smiling slightly. "Here's a rumor that's true: I used to cut myself."

"I heard that you were trying to commit suicide," Alric said. "I overheard a teacher from your school talking about it at church."

" Nurse Green saw me cutting myself in the bathroom at school and told one teacher at my high school who decided to tell the whole community that Nurse Green delivered me from suicide."

Alric chuckled and then sobered up. "What's the deal with you and David Hudson?"

Arnella pulled in a deep breath and straightened up on the chair. "That topic is off the table." She glanced at her watch. "I have to go."

Alric looked at her, confused, as she hurriedly stood up. Obviously that was a sore wound. He wished he hadn't brought it up. He had been enjoying getting to know Arnella.

"See you next class." She didn't look back to hear if he responded; she just left the classroom.

He steepled his fingers under his chin and thought about Arnella for the next few minutes. His mind barely concentrated on the class activity sheets that he had to mark. He was close to admitting that he liked her. For the life of him, he couldn't understand why.

Maybe it was the way she said "I am always unhappy." That touched a sympathetic chord within him.

*****

Arnella couldn't sleep, though she was in a queen sized bed that was more comfortable than any she had ever slept in. The temperature was just right—it was still chilly for summer, but not chilly enough that she had to get a blanket— yet she tossed and turned like a caged bird.

She looked at the clock. It was midnight. She had tried to go to bed early this evening so that she could paint early in the morning, but it was a no go. Her body was tired but not exhausted enough to sleep. She got up and glanced in the floor length mirror while passing it. She saw her messy hair and her puffy eyes and sighed. She was not looking too stellar for a twenty-year old. She looked trampled on. She headed out the door and to the landing. The place was quiet. Charlene had long gone to bed. She tiptoed down the hallway and down the stairs, entered the kitchen and headed for the fridge. A cup of hot milk would do her good. At least, it should help her sleep.

She closed her eyes briefly, and David's face loomed in her mind's eye. If only she could just blot it out of her mind that she was assaulted, but her mind was having none of it. She was no psychiatrist but she knew that this was the big reason for her restless sleep, especially since she saw David in class yesterday and knew that he and his cronies were on campus. Those creeps. If Alric hadn't intervened, she would surely have done some significant damage to David. She wished that kick she gave him yesterday could have broken him for life.

Maybe she needed to see Taj after all. She was willing to talk now. She felt so angry. She put the milk in the microwave and set the timer for 10 seconds. The timer went off in no time and she sipped the warm milk slowly, waiting for the soporific effects of the milk to kick in. When it didn't, she headed down to the basement, switching on all the lights and looked at her half finished work that was stacked in a corner.

She'd finish the sea scene first. She grabbed her newly bought paint, putting the milk on the worktable, and set up her canvas. What was it that Taj said he saw in the scene: despair and loneliness? She looked at it keenly. She was going to add some angry waves in the distance, making the painting even angrier than she had originally intended. She worked steadily through the night, eventually getting up from before the canvas when the first light of dawn was peeping through the skies. Painting, as usual, was cathartic. She went upstairs and saw Charlene rummaging in the kitchen.

"I thought I heard you down there last night," she said to Arnella brightly. "Couldn't sleep, huh?"

"No," Arnella said, shaking her head, "but I finished one piece of artwork. So maybe sleepless nights are not that bad."

"Would you like some breakfast?" Charlene asked.

"No, thanks. I am going to sleep. I have class in four hours. I may miss it as well as I may not."

Charlene laughed. "Don't let your uncle come and get you."

"I won't answer the door," Arnella said tiredly.

She went to her room and closed the door, drawing the curtains to block the sunlight. She closed her eyes and just could not fall asleep. Two hours later, she got up. She pulled on her favorite black sweater over her jeans and headed to the Psych Center. Maybe Taj was right after all. She really needed to talk about it.

*****

It was surprisingly easy to get an audience with Dr. Jackson, Arnella realized. Two minutes after driving up to the center and talking to the receptionist, she was sitting in front of Taj.

"You look like you didn't sleep last night," Taj said gently. 'Puffy red eyes and droopy lids."

Arnella twisted her hand. "I shouldn't have come by, but I have loads of things on my mind and you did say that your services are free."

Taj nodded. "I did and it is. I am glad you could stop by. What are some of the things you have on your mind?"

"Just stuff," Arnella sighed. "I have loads of things on my mind since childhood. I guess since my father died. I had a lousy time after his death."

Taj nodded. "Want to tell me about it?"

Arnella nodded. "Why not? It's not as if you are going to tell anybody? You are bound by law to keep my secrets, aren't you?"

Taj nodded slowly. "As long as you didn't kill anybody. I am obligated to report murder and child abuse."

Arnella chuckled. "You look so serious saying that. You know you are pretty cute. Too bad you are my cousin."

"Cute?" Taj frowned, "I haven't heard myself being described as cute since high school." He grinned. "You are deflecting. It's a pretty well known tactic that's used by patients who have something on their mind but don't want to talk. Remember I am not going to tell."

"I guess you've heard it all, huh?" Arnella asked. "This campus must be rife with secrets. Tell me some of them to make me comfortable."

Taj laughed. "You are testing me to see if I am going to share some with you."

Arnella shrugged, "It was worth a shot."

"A pretty obvious one," Taj said, looking at her. Arnella was a textbook case of a person in pain trying to pretend that she was tough. He looked at her perfectly symmetrical face and into her eyes. Even when she was laughing or pretending to be glib, there was a wealth of pain behind her eyes. He patiently waited for her to look around his office and then she looked back at him.

"That painting is ugly."

"Which one?" Taj looked behind him. It was an abstract of a brown vase with some sticks in it. It was meant to compliment the minimalism of the room and the soft earth tones in his office. He looked back at her. She was deflecting again.

"Who hurt you Arnella?" He asked frankly, focusing her attention to the here and now.

"I was drugged at a friend's party; some guys put something in some drinks. One of the sniveling cowards who did it said it was a bit of fun."

She closed her eyes and then swallowed. She wasn't ready to talk about it. Before Taj could react, she said quickly, "I had a good childhood till my father died when I was eight. You must have heard that Uncle Ryan had a brother, Oswald."

Taj nodded.

"Well, I was his favorite girl in the whole wide world. I knew my Daddy loved me and then he was gone. They said he died in a bar room brawl. Arnella cleared her throat. "Anyway, my mother fell apart when he died. She stopped living and started drinking. We were living in West Virginia at the time, and my brother and I used to go get her in the early mornings. Most times we would find her passed out on the streets in a ditch somewhere. One morning the local police saw us hauling her home, and they contacted social services. After the first visit, my mom decided that she had had enough of America and decided to come to Jamaica. She packed us up with one measly little suitcase a piece. She had one, Vanley had one, and I had one. My grandmother had a house out here and willed it to my Mom before she died, so we moved there."

Taj steepled his fingers, listening as Arnella painted a picture of her childhood. She was talking as if some of the details were long forgotten and she was bringing them back to mind.

She rested back in her chair and crossed her legs. "I had met Uncle Ryan in the past, you know, when Daddy was alive. Uncle Ryan used to live in Washington State. When we came to Jamaica, he was already out here. He thought we were just staying for vacation. He had no idea that my Mom was fleeing social services and the IRS and imminent institutionalization in a mental hospital."

She laughed dryly. "He found out, much later, what was going on and he sent Vanley to boarding school. My mother sobered up for a while, so I was left with her, but everything went down hill after that. She can't remember all the things she did to me because excessive alcohol abuse can cause holes in somebody's memory, but I remember. She used to starve me and beat me. One day she locked me in my room and forgot about me. I had to climb from the second story window. I was about ten...I ate out of the neighbor's garbage. I thought I was covering for her by not saying a word about how bad it was, not to my brother nor my uncle."

Taj just nodded. He didn't need to prompt her to talk. She just wanted to get things off her chest it seemed.

"I went looking for food one night, in the town, I was twelve. I was almost raped by a taxi driver. I am not new to sexual assaults. A stranger saved my butt then. I don't know why this current one should bother me so much. Yesterday I almost killed the guy that did this to me. He claimed that they raped me because of a dare."

"Do you want me to report this to the police?" Taj asked gently.

"I am not sure." Arnella shook her head. "I don't want this to be some big public thing and then there is no justice."

"They could do it to someone else," Taj said gently.

Arnella closed her eyes and leaned back in the chair. "I don't want to be a spectacle. I just want to be left alone. I feel so tired…"

Taj watched her for a minute, waiting for her to speak again, but when he heard a light snore, he smiled. He rarely had patients that fell asleep on him. He woke her up, "Arnella there is a room down the hall where you can sleep."

Arnella nodded dizzily. "Okay." He walked her to it and she fell on the bed. Soon she was off again. Taj told the nurses not to disturb her until evening.

Arnella woke up groggily to the ringing of her cell phone. At first, she had no idea where she was, and then she realized that she was still at the Psych Center. She looked on the call display. It was Tracy.

"Where are you, Nella? I heard the strangest news from David that you attacked him in class yesterday. Is it true?"

"Yes," Arnella's voice sounded husky and ill used, even to her ears. "I should have wrung his scrawny neck."

"But why?" Tracy asked puzzled. "I don't know you to be an angry person."

"He drugged me at your house and had sex with me without my consent." Arnella said sitting up in the bed and looking around.

"Are you sure Nella?" Tracy asked doubtfully. "You said this already but I can't really think of when they would have done that at the party."

Arnella stretched and put her feet on the floor. She yawned. "I know what I went through; I was not hallucinating. David was the main one in this whole sordid affair. I am going to get him."

"Now Nella, remember, nothing really bothers you." Tracy had a smug sound in her voice.

It made Arnella pause. It was almost as if Tracy was happy that she had been assaulted. She straightened her clothes. "Well, yipee for you. This one really bothers me."

"You sound like you need a little cheering up," Tracy said, changing the subject abruptly. "Want to go out later. You know, I haven't seen you since you've been up here. That's bad."

Arnella didn't want to go out, especially with Tracy. She felt tired and worn and strangely drained, as if talking to Taj had drained her vital energy. "I'll have to take a rain check on that."

"Well maybe this weekend then," Tracy said. "My club, InLaw, is having an oldies party, want to come?"

Arnella swallowed her denial. She was reluctant to go to any party ever again. "I might. I'll call you back," she said to Tracy reluctantly.

"Don't wait too long to tell me," Tracy said. "We have an RSVP guest list, and we are car pooling."

"Okay," Arnella hung up the phone and sat down on the

bed abruptly. She had let it all out on Taj earlier: her life, all the things she had bottled up and she was not even finished.

She realized that it hadn't even really been a session. She had just told him about her life and then fell asleep. She got up and peeped around the door. The carpeted hallway was empty. She headed to the sign that said 'lobby', and a nurse stopped her when she was about to leave.

"Dr. Jackson has set up a schedule for you." She handed Arnella a sheet of paper. "These are based on the breaks you have between classes. The sessions are twice weekly."

Arnella took the sheet of paper from her. "Wow, you guys are efficient."

The nurse smiled. "Don't be late for appointments."

Arnella nodded and headed outside.

Chapter Seven

Taj had had several patients during the day, but Arnella stood out in his mind. She was obviously battling with a list of problems that started from childhood. It was that kind of childhood setting that made him want to call his dad and Harriet and just talk.

They both knew how to raise children. They had raised him and he had not felt deprived even though he was adopted. He considered Ryan Bancroft to be his bonus father/friend whom he played squash with. His dad was his psychiatrist; he may not be trained, but he really knew how to give him good advice, solicited or not.

He was going through some tough decisions now. He was living with Jackie Beecher, platonically of course, though she had ramped up her come hither actions since she had signed a contract to be in Mount Faith for another year. At first, he had responded to the come-ons. He used to lightly flirt with her, especially when Natasha was away on some private detective case or the other. He had quickly rethought his attitude to Jackie and had sorted out his misguided feelings for her. All he wanted now was to be with Natasha. She had one course left to graduate with her master's degree in Forensic Psychology and then he would pop the question.

He pushed his hand into his pocket and felt the ring box. Maybe he should do it now, before she finishes in December. He had been treating Jackie distantly, and she had ramped up the vamp.

He opened his front door and was immediately bombarded with the scent of incense. Jackie was draped across the sofa. Her long hair was brushed out and flowing over one arm. Her lips were painted mulberry red, and she was listening to mood music. Her red negligee revealed one bare arm.

He paused at the door and raised his eyebrows. "Jackie. I hope I am not interrupting anything."

"Oh, hi," Jackie said to him breezily. "I am unwinding, easing the tension of the day."

Taj grinned. "Okay, let me not interrupt."

"No," Jackie said, getting up, her sultry pout replaced with a plea. "Please stay. I need to talk. "

Taj sighed and sat down across from her. "I'm all ears."

"I think Natasha is wrong for you," Jackie said softly.

Taj shook his head. "I can't think why."

"She has a black belt in some strange Asian discipline. She'll break your neck if you two have an argument and nobody is around."

Jackie adjusted her negligee top to show more skin, looking at Taj while she did it. Seeing no visible softening of his eyes on her, she hissed her teeth. "You are so controlled. Unnaturally so."

Taj leaned back in his chair. "It's called dissociation. This one is mild detachment. One develops it over time, dealing with patients."

"Taj, I'm not a patient," Jackie said, frustrated with him. "You liked me one time. I could see it. Don't deny it. You were softening toward me. What caused this coldness?"

"For one crazy moment, well maybe a month, I thought about being with you." Taj shrugged. "I wouldn't have been human if I hadn't. You are really gorgeous and I am a healthy heterosexual male."

"Thanks," Jackie preened. "So what changed?"

"I love how you look, but I love Natasha, all of her, even when she's grumpy. I can't shake it; she's the one."

"But she is always away on some covert mission or the other," Jackie said pouting, "She thinks that her career is more important than your relationship. That, in my opinion, is a deal breaker."

Taj laughed. "Isn't that why you and Gareth divorced?"

"Yes," Jackie smirked, "but see, I learned my lesson. I am now more aware of what to do in a relationship. I am a far better option than Natasha right now because she hasn't learned that lesson yet."

The doorbell rang and Taj raised his eyebrows at Jackie. "Expecting somebody?"

Jackie shrugged. "No. You?"

Taj shook his head and got up. Jackie reclined on the sofa and smiled wickedly when she heard Natasha's voice at the front door.

"You left a message at the front desk of my building saying that you wanted to see me." Natasha hugged Taj. "That's so sweet. I thought you said you had a whole lot of paperwork and..." Her voice trailed off when she came into the living room and saw Jackie in lingerie, smiling benignly.

Taj had a perplexed look on his face.

"What is it, detective?" Jackie asked, purring, "You look

shell-shocked." She arched her back seductively. "You really can't barge into our mutual dwelling without warning, you know. You just might interrupt something private."

Natasha sat down in the chair across from Jackie and chuckled. "Taj hates incense; reminds him of his mother's funeral. Aren't you tired of the staged seduction scenes? I am not as gullible as Kylie, you know. She told me the story of your little bid to get between her and Gareth."

Jackie sighed and got up. "It was worth a shot." She swung her hair back in frustration, "I am not really an evil villain, as everybody is making me out to be, you know, including that milk-mouthed Kylie."

Natasha chuckled, "I believe you."

Jackie snarled. "Don't sympathize with me. You have no idea how hard I worked to get Taj to give you up."

Natasha shook her head and watched as Jackie flounced to her room.

"You better marry her fast Taj, or you are fair game." Jackie looked at him soulfully and then slammed her door.

Taj sighed and sat down beside Natasha. "She's right." He felt in his pocket and took out the ring box he had been carrying around for days. He removed the ring. "Tash, I love you. Will you marry me?"

Natasha giggled. "Love you too, and of course I'll marry you."

She kissed him on the lips and then drew back and looked him in the eyes. "We are not going to be living here with Jackie, are we?"

Taj shook his head vehemently. "Oh, no. I will have to sort out something."

Chapter Eight

The weekend came too quickly for Arnella. She was just getting into the groove of school. Tracy called Arnella as soon as she stepped into Computer 101, her final class on Friday morning and her final class for the week. It was in the Information Science building.

"Arnella, you haven't gotten back to me about that party." Tracy was in her apartment filing her nails. "It's Saturday night you know. I have to give my friends some feedback today."

Arnella grimaced; she had completely forgotten about Tracy and her party. "I can't," Arnella said, taking her seat at a computer that was at the back. "I have stuff to do."

Truth was, she didn't want to hang out with Tracy, and she had her art to do. She was itching to finish a painting for Taj that she had started. She saw that he liked earth tones so she was doing an abstract for him for his office. It could double as an engagement present as well. He told her, at their session yesterday, that he had proposed to Natasha.

"Stuff?" Tracy asked, a sneer in her voice. What could be more important than hanging out with her? Everyday she was getting increasingly curious about Arnella. She realized that Arnella was drawing herself away from her, and that bothered her.

"Yup, stuff." Arnella turned on her computer. "I have to go; my teacher is here." Arnella hung up the phone, wishing she hadn't lied to Tracy. Her teacher was not there yet, but she was tired of Tracy.

She checked her email account and saw an email from a strange address with the caption "I know what you did at the party."

Her hands started to tremble and her heart started pounding in her chest. She didn't want to open it. She stared at the screen for so long that her eyes started to water.

"Hey," said an older lady who was sitting beside her. "You look like you know computers well. I am going to need some help to get through this class. I am hopeless. My name is Sadie. What's yours?"

Arnella cleared her throat and dragged her eyes from the screen. "Arnella." She smiled, or at least she hoped the corners of her mouth lifted into a smile because Sadie looked like a pleasant lady.

She put both hands in her lap and willed them to stop shaking. Then, taking a deep breath, she clicked on the mail. There was a message; it was brief and read, "Bad bad girl." Below it was a video clip. She knew that she shouldn't play the video clip in the class, but she was itching to see it nevertheless.

The teacher finally arrived ten minutes late, but when she spoke, Arnella didn't hear a word. She had the window open with the email, and she kept going back to it. From just looking at the message, she was breathing hard; she could hear it in her own ears. She felt like passing out from the fear of what was in that video. It had to be a clip from the party. Was it with her and those guys? Her left foot kept jumping, and she couldn't stop the involuntary action. She kept glancing at the clock, waiting for the hour-long class to be over. She almost sobbed in relief when class was over.

"Are you okay dear?" Sadie asked her, concerned. "You don't have asthma, do you?"

"No," Arnella said weakly. "I just don't feel too well."

"Want me to follow you to the school nurse, or to the Medical Center?" Sadie persisted.

"No, thanks," Arnella said weakly. "My cousin, Kylie, is a lecturer here; I am going to see her. She'll know what to do."

"Okay then." Sadie reluctantly left her and Arnella realized that her trembling hands were icy cold. Even the bulk sweater she had carried to wear in the lab was not doing anything for her cold extremities.

She was shivering. She looked at the mail again, then pressed the play button on the video. It was a picture of her in the swimming pool when she was floating on the donut and calling to Alric; the video zoomed into her tongue ring. There was a song playing in the background. She almost released a sigh, but then the transitioned and she saw herself passionately kissing David. The video blacked out and the words "More to Come" flashed on the screen.

The tremor in her hand came back with a vengeance. She inhaled but couldn't get in enough breaths. Those hudlums had video taped her and had the nerve to send it to her. She sat in the lab with her hand over head for what seemed like hours. Students came in to use the lab; she could hear murmurings and sometimes the odd laugh or cough, but she couldn't move.

"Arnella," Gareth Beecher said above her head.

Arnella shook her head.

"I know it is you," Gareth said. "Why are you hiding around here?"

Arnella looked at him blearily. She had closed her eyes so tightly that when she opened them she had to let them adjust to the light.

Gareth was looking at her, concerned. "Come to my office now."

Arnella didn't want to move; maybe if she stayed still long enough he would go away, but Gareth was standing above her, not moving an inch. She got up reluctantly. She felt like an ancient grandmother who had the world on her shoulders. She double-checked to make sure that her mail account was closed and followed Gareth to his office.

When they reached his office, she saw Kylie sitting in his chair. She looked concerned when she saw Arnella.

"What's wrong, cuz?" Kylie asked, looking from Arnella to Gareth.

Gareth shrugged. "She was in the back of the computer lab whimpering."

Kylie got up, closed the office door, came over to Arnella, and hugged her. "It's okay, whatever it is."

Arnella shook her head. "I got an email." Her lips were trembling.

"From who?" Kylie asked, brushing away stray tendrils of hair from her face.

"I don't know," Arnella said. "It said 'bad bad girl. I know what you did at the party.'" She swallowed. "I was drugged a couple of weeks ago and three guys had sex with me. Apparently, they videotaped it. Now it seems as if somebody is toying with me."

Kylie gasped. "What!"

Gareth, who had just sat down in his chair, looked at Arnella with surprise. He and Kylie exchanged shocked looks.

"We have to tell the police," Kylie said without preamble. She took out her cell phone.

"No!" Arnella said, slumping into the chair nearest to her. "Please no. I just need to know who is sending the email."

"Who are the guys who did this to you?" Kylie asked urgently. "You have to tell us."

"They went to my high school and now they are up here," Arnella said, "I thought about telling the police too but the thing is, it's my word against their's."

She exhaled tremulously. "I can't believe this is happening to me. Well, maybe I can, I knew something bad was going to happen to me after I moved into Deidra's place. Good things just don't happen to me without bad things following on its heels to make me unhappy. I can never catch a break. Never!"

She bit her lip and then stood up shakily. "I have to go."

"Ah, honey don't go," Kylie said gently. "We need to talk about this."

"Is it possible these guys are the ones sending you the video?" Gareth asked, "Because that could be evidence. I mean, I could ask Jackie..."

"No Jackie," Kylie said fiercely. "We have our own family detective. Natasha and Taj are engaged; she's practically family. She's a police detective; we could talk to her about this. Don't you dare think you are alone in this, Nella."

Kylie hugged her tightly. "There has to be some justice in this for you."

Arnella got up. "Thanks guys for caring, but I am just going to go now."

Kylie nodded. "Want to come to church with me and Gareth tomorrow?"

"No." Arnella shook her head. "Vanley and Aunt Celeste already invited me. I am going to just chill tomorrow, okay?"

"Okay." Kylie watched her leave and then shook her head at Gareth. "Whoever is messing with Nella doesn't know that they're messing with the Bancroft family. When my Dad hears this he is going to flip."

*****

Alric sat around the church organ in the University Church for Sabbath worship. From his vantage point, he could see the whole church. The Bancrofts were sitting en masse to his right. He kept glancing over there to see if he could see Arnella. She had not come in with the rest of her family. He had been expecting her to be here today because her brother Vanley was doing his debut sermon. It was his first time speaking as an assistant pastor of the University Church. All the other Bancrofts were there to offer their support.

He wondered why Arnella was not there. Was she so totally against church that she didn't want to even attend once to give familial encouragement?

He looked across at Vanley, who was sitting in the preacher's chair. He didn't look nervous, or like he needed support. He looked like a man who had a message and was chomping at the bit to deliver it.

Alric's mind wandered back to Arnella. He almost missed the cue to start the music for the opening song "A Mighty Fortress Is Our God".

After the song, he wondered if Arnella was sick or something. That could be her reason for not attending. In class on Wednesday, she had been majorly subdued and she had hightailed it out of the class before he could say anything to her. She hadn't even looked at him. It had bothered him for the entire day.

He forcibly dragged his mind from Arnella and focused on the proceedings. It wasn't until the service was finished that he acknowledged to himself that he had not succeeded in keeping Arnella out of his mind.

Vanley had delivered a powerful sermon on prophecy and the signs of the times, but he had been staring at him and wondering how he could have a sibling that was so radically different from him—so troubled and unhappy. Vanley didn't seem as if he had any hang ups like that. He was a well-respected young pastor at the university. He was so upright and straitlaced that even his own father, a minister of religion for over thirty years, spoke fondly of him and respected him implicitly.

He almost bumped into Tracy when he left the platform where the organ was. She had been standing at the base of the steps and was smiling at him.

"Oh sorry, Tracy, didn't see you there." Alric smiled at her. "You look lovely today." He admired her in her blue suit and matching hat.

"Thank you," Tracy smiled. "How are you? I can't believe we live in the same apartment complex and I don't ever see you."

Alric smiled. "That's because I am a working student. Final year med school with one lab to teach affords me hardly time to sleep."

He headed toward the door where the platform party was lined up shaking the hands of the membership. Tracy shuffled behind him, trying to keep up in her high heels. He slowed down so that she could catch up.

"So where are you having lunch today?" She asked when she caught up with him.

Alric shrugged; he was thinking of having lunch with his

parents, but a little part of him wanted to see if Arnella was all right.

"My parents, probably." Then the thought hit him. Arnella and Tracy were friends; maybe Tracy would know where Arnella was.

"By the way, have you seen Arnella today? I thought that with her brother preaching today she would have shown up for church."

Tracy stopped abruptly. The guy behind her almost walked into her. "What?" she asked, open-mouthed. "Vanley Bancroft is related to Arnella?"

Alric raised one eyebrow. "Yes. Are you sure you guys are friends? How come you didn't know this?"

"Well, I..." Tracy frowned, "but President Bancroft is Vanley's uncle."

Alric chuckled. "Yes."

"So Arnella is that closely related to them?"

Alric nodded.

Tracy covered her mouth. "I feel so foolish. I thought she was distantly related you know, like a third cousin or something. Arnella doesn't act as if they are closely related.

"Do you know where she's living?" Alric asked.

Tracy shrugged, "I am not sure, she said something about Buena Vista."

Alric opened his eyes wide. "That's a nice place. I know where it is."

"It is?" Tracy asked faintly. Then she cleared her throat. "Why do you want to know where she lives?"

"I am a bit concerned about her," Alric said. "She didn't seem like herself in class on Wednesday, and she wasn't here for her brother's sermon. It was his first presentation."

"But you hate her," Tracy said, dismayed. She could care less about it being Vanley's first sermon. "You hate her, remember?" she said frantically.

"Keep your voice down," Alric whispered. They were standing near the door outside of foot traffic. The line toward the door was getting shorter as more people filed out. Some persons had looked around as Tracy blurted out the word 'hate'.

"I don't hate her," Alric said uncomfortably, "I think she's unhappy, and I am concerned."

"Unhappy?" Tracy's eyes widened. "Arnella is always happy and carefree. Where'd you get that from?"

Alric frowned. Obviously, Tracy didn't know Arnella as well as she thought. He shrugged. "I am just concerned… basic concern. I am going to check up on her at Buena Vista."

"I am coming with you." Tracy declared staunchly. "She's my friend. I didn't know she was unhappy." The last bit was said in almost a pleased tone.

*****

Arnella had been in the basement painting when she heard the door buzzer going off. She wanted to ignore it but it could be somebody stopping by for Charlene. She looked down at her paint-spattered jeans shorts and her once white t-shirt and shrugged. She would just send whoever it was on their way when they found out that Charlene had gone to church.

She got up from her chair, stretched, and headed upstairs. She spoke into the intercom, "Charlene is not here."

"I came to see you, actually." Alric retorted.

Arnella closed her eyes and swallowed. "Arnella is not here either," she said gruffly. "She will be back on Monday."

"Ah, come on," Alric said, "I drove all the way up here to see you. By the way, Tracy is here with me. We were both concerned about you."

Arnella straightened up when she heard that Tracy was there. For a nanosecond, when her brain had skipped a process, she had liked the thought of Alric coming to see her. Thank God her brain was functioning again because she didn't want her mind thinking that she liked Alric.

"Okay," she said grumpily and opened the gate.

She defiantly looked at herself in the mirror. She was not going to change. They were the ones who were visiting her. She didn't ask them to.

Her hair had green paint on the tips and was a shaggy mess. She opened the front door and stood in the opening as Alric got out the car, waving to her as he went to open Tracy's door.

Who said chivalry was dead? Arnella thought snarkily, but a piece of her, the part that she thought hadn't gone all bad, admired Alric's old-fashioned manners. If she were to be honest, she admired him. He looked handsome in his dark-gray suit. He was clean-shaven, and his hair was growing back from the completely bald look. Tracy stood beside him when she came out of the car, deliberately pressing closer to him than was necessary Arnella thought.

Alric eased back from her quickly. Arnella grinned; in a flash she summed up his feelings toward Tracy. It was not encouraging. *Poor rich Tracy.*

"I told him nothing was wrong with you," Tracy said, looking over at her. "See, you look happy."

Arnella laughed a forced sound that sounded fake, even to her own ears. "Why would you think something was wrong with me, Alric? I am fine."

"Your brother preached at church today, his first time in the pulpit for the semester. I thought you would have come for that."

Arnella shrugged. Vanley had begged her to come, and she

would have, if she had not been so rattled by the video in her email. She hadn't slept since she watched it. She had been in the basement all night painting. She wouldn't tell Alric that though, especially since Tracy was there.

She looked up at Alric; he had walked up to and stood close in front of her. He towered over her, his tall muscular frame almost daunting. He smelled good too. Her eyes connected with his, and for the life of her, she couldn't shift her eyes from the stare. He was reading her; his eyes were burrowing into hers, trying to ferret out her secrets. She tried to break the contact but it held her there. It was magnetic, almost other-worldly.

"Nice place," Tracy said brightly, looking between the two of them with a puzzled expression.

Alric dragged his eyes from Arnella's first, and she blinked. "Yes, er thanks. It's Deidra's place."

"Deidra Durkheim!" Tracy squealed. "You know her?"

"Yeah," Arnella said. "She is married to Marcus. So technically she is a Bancroft now."

"You dark horse you," Tracy said, shreds of envy in her tone. "You never told me you were so closely related to the Bancrofts."

Arnella shrugged, "I am. Come on in, since you are already here." She looked back at Alric, who was looking at her with his eyebrows raised mockingly.

She indicated to the living room and Tracy followed her, gasping in awe. "This place looks amazing."

"Yes, it is," Arnella said." Would you guys like lunch? Charlene has the fridge stocked with food."

"Who is Charlene?" Tracy asked the question she had been dying to ask.

"Deidra's sister," Arnella replied abruptly. She was beginning to regret their intrusion into her day.

"Yes, I would like some food," Alric said. "I was planning to eat at my parents but having lunch with you would be as good."

Arnella opened her mouth to tell him that he wasn't having lunch with her, but then closed it. She needed to be gracious Alric had really saved her life the other day when he invited her to his mother's birthday lunch. He had also possibly saved her from jail when she attacked David.

So, she put on her best hostess smile and took out Charlene's cooked food. She even made vegetables and a fruit salad. All the while Tracy was talking a mile a minute, asking her questions about her family.

"I can't believe that you personally know Marcus Bancroft," Tracy said enviously.

Arnella shrugged, "Marcus and I were adversaries when we were younger. We used to fight a lot when I came to stay for the holidays. He had this thing about girls playing with each other and boys doing their own thing. I begged to differ. I loved playing with the boys."

Alric looked at her sharply when she said that, and she grinned, carrying the food over to the table. "Bon appetit."

"Aren't you going to eat?" Alric asked as she sat down with them.

"No." Arnella shook her head. "No appetite."

Alric cleared his throat. Having Tracy there was preventing him from asking Arnella what was wrong. She was not her usual self. He didn't even know how he knew that something was wrong or what her usual self was; he just knew. He also knew that she had on her armor. He could see that her smiles weren't genuine. They were brittle, as if one little shove in the wrong direction would make her break down crying.

Her eyes looked tired, and behind the laughs and the talk was a sense of unhappiness. He also concluded that Arnella didn't want Tracy to know that she had on this armor. It was a puzzle to him that he was finding it so easy to read her. Maybe when she confessed to him that she was unhappy he had started looking beyond the surface.

"Vanley did a beautiful sermon today," he said aloud, digging into the meal.

"I knew he would," Arnella said wryly. "He has preached to me enough times for met to know that he is a good preacher."

Tracy was watching her, a bitterness twisting her lips. "I can't believe that I didn't know you were his sister. I have known you for seven years and not once did you say anything." Tracy shook her head, "I had a crush on Marcus Bancroft. Remember? You never said he was your cousin."

Arnella laughed. "It's not a big deal. I don't know your extended family, do I?"

Tracy narrowed her eyes. "Really, Arnella? There is nobody interesting in my family. I told you last year that President Bancroft gave me and some other freshmen special attention when he invited us to the president's ball. You never said a word that he was your uncle, even when I was applying up here and I was telling you all about Mount Faith...I can't believe this."

Arnella looked at Alric; his eyes were alight looking from her to Tracy. She smiled at him slightly.

Are you okay? He mouthed to her.

She looked away. She had some very angry and lonely paintings downstairs to prove it. She had gone on a painting spree to vent her emotions.

Alric looked her over. Her paint-spattered blouse was crumbled and she had bits of paint clinging to her hair ends. She still looked beautiful to him though, almost childish. Make up free, piercing free, she was au natural. He felt like rubbing off the splatter of green paint she had on her cheek.

"Want to come back to church with us?" he asked Arnella. Tracy had stopped talking and was sulking beside him. "You look like you could do with the company."

"I am okay," Arnella said. "I don't mind my own company."

"Oh, that's right," Tracy piped in. "You consider yourself to be this creative genius who loves her own company and doesn't have to tell her friend anything."

Arnella winced. She was finding Tracy increasingly annoying by the minute.

Alric got up. "Come on, Tracy. Let's go. Thanks for lunch, Arnella. Tell Charlene that she is a good cook."

"But I want to stay," Tracy said looking at Arnella. "I am pretty sure Arnella doesn't mean me when she says she loves her own company."

Arnella threw a look of desperation to Alric and he laughed inwardly. The dynamics had obviously changed between Arnella and Tracy.

Chapter Nine

"**I** can't believe that Arnella is living in that house," Tracy said incredulously. "I can't believe it."

Alric looked back at the gate as it closed. "Why is it so hard to believe?" he asked Tracy, who seemed to be fuming.

"She didn't say a word to me that she was related to them. I don't know what to think right now."

"Maybe she didn't want to boast. Not everybody is a name dropper," Alric said softly. "Arnella is a different specie. I'm getting to understand that she's proud, independent, and stubborn."

"Why are you talking as if you like her?" Tracy asked suspiciously. "Remember you told me that she was bad news and I shouldn't be friends with her?"

"I have since rethought that." Alric shrugged. "She is surprisingly different from what I heard about her when we were growing up. Some of the rumors that I heard about her, I have since found to be untrue. I am now wondering if some views I've had about her over the years are untrue as well."

Tracy gasped. "They are true. She is just good at spinning tales to justify herself. Don't listen to her."

Alric frowned. They were nearing the university campus. "I thought you guys were friends. Why the sudden about face?"

"Every guy I introduce Arnella to has always been captivated under her spell except for you. Do you know what she does with guys I like?" Tracy's lip trembled. "She sleeps with them and then she tells me about it. She calls it the Arnella test. She knows that I like you Alric. So if you don't mind being a notch on her bedpost you better watch out."

Alric slowed down at the entrance to Mount Faith; his hand tightened on the steering wheel. "Church or home?" he asked Tracy, processing the information he just heard.

"Home," Tracy said heavily.

Alric drove toward Blue Palm Apartments, his mind ticking over. *Arnella and her over zealous sexuality again.* Was she that free with her favors? He felt uncomfortably, angry, and bitter. It's as if every time he thought about giving Arnella a chance, he heard awful things about her.

He drove up to the apartment, which was painted in a dark blue with white trimmings and palms artfully arranged near the building.

"So where on the complex do you live?" Tracy asked curiously. "You know, I never see you around here."

Her heart was singing. Alric had looked disgusted when she had told him about Arnella. *That was how it should be; how dare him like Arnella? This should have him avoiding her for life. He was a guy of principles. Guys like Alric did not date Arnella. Nobody wanted a whore for a wife.*

"I live on block F." Alric put the car in park and looked at Tracy. "You know, something baffles me."

"What?" Tracy asked eagerly, ready to answer any questions about Arnella with more damning information.

"How is it that Arnella sleeps with guys you like and you are still friends with her? Isn't that taking friendship a bit far? I mean..."

"I am still friends with her because I thought she was poor and in need of some sort of support. She doesn't have many friends, you know. I couldn't bear to leave her alone. So, I've forgiven her time and time again. Now I am finding out that she was not as destitute as she made herself out to be. I feel so used."

"How many guys have you introduced to Arnella and she slept with them?" Alric asked, searching Tracy's face for any hint of a lie.

"Six," Tracy said without hesitation. "She's been at it from high school." She shrugged. "Maybe you will be number seven."

Alric sighed. "Not on your life."

Tracy exhaled happily. That was said with such conviction that she was actually giddy with exhilaration. Alric probably hated Arnella very much right now. "Want to come up to my apartment. I am on block A."

Alric shook his head ruefully. "No. I have to do something now." He got out of the car and opened her door. "See you around."

Tracy scrambled out of the car, reluctant to see him leave. "Do you want to go to a party with me tonight? It's a law club thing."

"No." Alric shook his head. "I am spending the night in the library. Final year...no time to even scratch my head. Take care, Tracy."

*****

Alric went to the medical library as soon as it opened at sunset. He had gone to his apartment and tried to reconcile the two Arnella's in his head: the one who was a nymphomaniac and slept with every guy that crossed her path, and the one who seemed unhappy and vulnerable, the one he was unaccountably attracted to. He needed to stop obsessing over Arnella. He couldn't afford to, and didn't want to. She was and would always be bad news for him.

The library was eerily quiet; most persons were not spending their Saturday nights studying. He ran his hand over his face, pulled out his phone, and put it on top of his textbook. Was Tracy really telling the truth about her?

He tapped his fingers on the desk. She slept with six guys and then had the gall to tell Tracy the details. He had doubts about that story, especially the part about him being number seven. Arnella did not act as if she liked him at all, nor did she give him any signals that she was even remotely interested in him. So, what was wrong with him then? The little thought crept into his head and lodged in his mind.

He opened his first-year book on Metabolism. He needed some information for his final project and he needed a refresher from his freshman and junior year courses. He looked through the books trying to get lost in them, but ended up staring balefully at his phone.

He wanted to talk to Arnella. He had taken her number from the first class where the names and numbers of each student were recorded for future reference. Her number was the only one he had memorized. He punched in the numbers reluctantly and was about to hang up after the third ring. What was he doing?

"Hello," Arnella's voice floated through the airwaves and into his ear. He almost hung up.

"It's me," he said simply. "I am in the medical library thinking about you. I don't know why."

Arnella was silent. He was actually tensing up to hear the dial tone in his ear. "I am in the basement painting a picture," she said after a long pause.

"It's Saturday night," Alric said. "This is ridiculous: me in the library, you in your basement."

Arnella chuckled. "What would you be doing if you weren't at the library?"

"That's easy, in my apartment watching this movie I have been dying to see. Have you ever seen Okike's Calling? It's about this young guy from Africa whose dream is to become a doctor, but he's really poor. I saw the preview and liked it."

"No, never seen it." Arnella cleared her throat and then hesitantly asked. "If you have it on DVD you can come watch it with me. Charlene is gone to Micah's place so I am home alone."

Alric could feel his fingers tightening on the phone. Was this a come on? Was he going to see Arnella in action? Was he going to be her next victim? The thought filled him with dread, disappointment, and a curious excitement.

"Okay. I'll be by in thirty minutes." He packed up his books and hurriedly shoved them into his backpack.

*****

He made the journey in twenty-five minutes, and when he drove up the curving driveway he wondered, not for the first time, what kind of mad experiment he was conducting with Arnella. What if she really was the vamp that Tracy insisted she was, did he have the willpower to resist her since he liked her so much?

When she opened the front door, he was fully expecting

her to be as unkempt as she was in the morning, but she was in sweat pants and a long sleeved shirt and she had her hair neatly brushed into a ponytail.

"Don't blame me if I sleep on you," Arnella said jokingly when he walked behind her into the living room. "I haven't slept in a while, and I doubt you and I will have the same taste in movies."

Alric cleared his throat. "Well, let's see."

She pointed to the DVD player and he put it in.

"Want something to eat?" Arnella asked.

"No, thanks." Alric studied her features intently." Have you gotten back your appetite yet? Today you said you had no appetite."

Arnella shook her head and sat in the settee. "No. Not back yet."

"What's wrong?" Alric took the remote in his hand and lowered the volume.

"It's nothing much." Arnella swallowed. "I guess I am extra sensitive about something right now. My appetite will come back."

"Or maybe you are pregnant?" Alric said softly. "You know, that is a consequence of sleeping around."

Arnella inhaled sharply. "I don't sleep around, and I am sure I am not pregnant."

Alric swallowed. He wanted to attack her with what Tracy, her closest friend, told him but he just shrugged. "Okay, if you're sure."

"I am sure. Play the DVD," Arnella said, curling up in a ball at one end of the couch. He was sitting at the other end.

"Do you like me?" he blurted out while the opening credits were going on.

"No," Arnella sniggered. "I have no interest in you whatsoever."

"So, why did you allow me to come over here?" Alric asked, a little spark of rejection hitting him.

"I wanted company," Arnella said, looking at him, "and you were the only one who called me. I was tired of my own thoughts, and I just wanted to talk to someone who wasn't a Bancroft."

"I get you." Alric nodded. "And you are boyfriend-less at this time."

"I have never had a boyfriend." Arnella looked at the screen.

"What? Never?" Alric's eyes widened. "That's unbelievable."

Arnella chuckled. "And flies in the face of everything you think you know about me."

"Well," Alric paused the show, "are you serious?"

Arnella nodded. "Yes, I find the dating ritual to be tedious. Besides, I have never met anybody who was worth losing my head over."

"So how does it work for you? You just say hi to a guy that you like and then have sex with him?" Alric asked slowly, really interested in hearing her answer.

Arnella rubbed her nose and giggled. "I doubt women do that, except as a job."

"Then..." Alric had so many questions in his head about her. They were almost choking him.

"Are we going to watch the movie?" Arnella asked. She clutched the pillow in her arms, and he suddenly wished he were the pillow.

He nodded. "Sure."

They watched the movie, which was a tearjerker. Arnella was sniffing through the whole thing.

"Tell anybody you saw me cry and you are a dead man," she said when the final credits started rolling.

Alric grinned. "With that threat, I won't."

"So what about you?" Arnella asked after a long pause. "Why are you girlfriend-less?"

Alric shrugged. "I have a girlfriend; her name is Medicine."

Arnella grinned. "Tracy will be quite jealous to hear that."

"Tell me about Tracy. You guys seem to have a strange friendship."

"About Tracy." Arnella rubbed her forehead. "Let's see. She's beautiful, rich, comes from a healthy family background, has two older brothers, a banker for a father..."

"No," Alric shook his head, "I mean what kind of person is she?"

Arnella shrugged. "She is friendly, ambitious..."

"You like her, don't you?" Alric asked earnestly. "You must like her a lot to do the Arnella test on prospective boyfriends."

"Arnella test?" Arnella sat up in the settee. "What's that?"

"When Tracy likes a guy, she introduces you to them. If she likes them, you sleep with them to test their loyalty."

Arnella's slightly damp eyes were blinking at him as if he had two heads. "I have never done anything like that in my life."

Alric got up. "Tracy told me that you have done it with six guys already, and she cautioned me that I am the seventh."

Arnella lay back down in the settee, clutched the cushion even closer to her, and said weakly, "That's a shocker."

"What's a shocker?" Alric stooped down before her. "Talk to me."

They stared at each other and then Arnella closed her eyes. "Do you believe her?"

"I don't want to," Alric said. "I was so jealous today when I heard. I was just about getting over seeing you with those three guys at her party, and now this. I don't want to like you

Arnella, but I can't help it. This feeling. It's confusing and crazy and exciting and dreadful all rolled into one."

"There is no Arnella test," she said quietly. She had no energy to defend her already battered reputation. "And I wished that you never told me how you felt about me."

Alric ran his finger over her downy soft cheekbone. "Why?"

Arnella's breath hitched at the contact. "Because I don't want a relationship. I don't want to care about you."

Alric leaned closer to her. "What about friendship, pure platonic friendship? I'll have to work this crazy feeling out of my system somehow. Maybe the more I get to know you, the more abhorrent you will become."

Arnella chuckled. "Okay. I can work with that; friendship it is."

Chapter Ten

Arnella almost missed her Computer 101 class on Monday. She had slept most of Sunday, and it had rained in the morning. She had not wanted to get out of bed. Besides, she was dreading going around anything with technology. What if she opened her email and saw another message with a video attached?

When she entered the lobby of the Computer Science building, she saw Kylie waving to her vigorously.

"I have class," Arnella said to her cousin, who was smartly dressed in a black suit. "Where are you off to?"

"I am off to Kingston to present a prototype of a new game Gareth and I developed. Before I forget, I spoke to Natasha."

Arnella sighed.

"I gave her your number. You had better talk to her about this. I also told Dad."

"What?" Arnella hissed. "Why'd you do that?"

"Because those louses who did this to you come to his

university. Dad is going to be off the island for two weeks. He said he'll deal with it when he gets back."

Arnella hung her head. "My shame is complete."

"You have nothing to be ashamed about," Kylie said taking her hands gently. "You love to carry everything around with you too much. We want to help, okay? We are your family."

Arnella nodded and then swallowed. "Thanks, I guess."

"Natasha said she'd call you tonight." Kylie squeezed Arnella's hand and walked away.

Arnella headed to class, cringing inwardly at her uncle finding out about her being violated. She didn't like anybody knowing, but her uncle was another matter... that made her feel strange.

She slipped into the back of the lab, beside Saidie. The teacher was already there. She was handing out an assignment. Arnella took the paper from her and then signed onto the computer.

"You look better today," Saidie whispered to her.

She smiled. "Thanks, I am better...had an okay weekend."

Well, better than okay. She had hung out with Alric for all of Saturday night. They had talked and talked until Charlene had arrived home late in the night. By Sunday morning, she had decided that she definitely liked him. It was still a surprise to her that he was so down to earth and cool. She had even been tempted to show him her art collection. She never felt the urge to do that with anyone.

She clicked on her email and scrolled through. There was an email from Deidra about the progress of the bags and then there was one from a strange address: EasterBunny@mail. com. This time, it was entitled. "Bad girls can't hide." It had a video attached.

Arnella bit her lip. She would not open another one of them alone again.

"So do you know how to do basic programming?" Saidie asked her as she looked down on the paper. "Why do they have all of these weird commands?"

Arnella forced herself to focus on the paper in front of her but the mail was on her mind. Who could be doing this to her? She was sure it was the first question Natasha would ask. She thought about it all through class. She had David, Cody, and Jeff as the top contenders. David had admitted that they had done a video and destroyed it. How did they destroy it? Had they even destroyed it?

When class was finally over, she walked to the Business Center toward the Student Lounge. She started to panic, wondering who else had seen the video and what exactly was on it. She could vaguely remember details about that day. She sat down dejectedly in the middle of the courtyard. She had a session with Taj tomorrow but wished it were today.

"You are a hard sister to find," Vanley said behind her. He touched her on the shoulder warmly and then sat beside her.

"Vanley!" Arnella grinned.

"Don't act like you are happy to see me," Vanley said reprovingly. "I begged you to come hear me preach on Sabbath and you didn't."

"I was depressed," Arnella said. I just wanted to be alone. Besides, I don't like church. I have no idea why you like it so much that you are actually planning to spend the rest of your life as the head of one? It must be the craziest job in the world."

Vanley sat beside her. As usual, he was dressed semi-formally. She hugged him when he sat down and sniffed him. "You smell nice."

"You okay?" Vanley looked down into her eyes. He had in contacts and they enhanced his light brown eyes. As usual, those eyes were forcing her to tell the truth.

"No." Arnella shook her head. It always irked her that she could not lie to Vanley for long. "I am seeing a psychiatrist though. "

Vanley squeezed her shoulders. "Do you want to talk to your big brother about it?"

"Nah." Arnella shuddered. "It would feel too weird."

"Do you want us to tell Jesus about it?" Vanley asked her gazing down at her, a quirk to his lips.

"What? Now?" Arnella asked surprised. "There are people around."

"There is nobody near us." Vanley shrugged. "They won't hear us."

"I can't pray in public," Arnella said urgently. "Are you crazy?"

Vanley chuckled. "Want to pray in private?"

"No," Arnella said, getting uncomfortable. "What does Jesus know about me? Nothing. He doesn't care. I am not going to be talking to your imaginary friend called Jesus."

Vanley sighed and patted her hand. "Can you do something for me?"

"What?" Arnella asked cautiously. Her brother was known to be gently persuasive.

"I am not knocking your psychiatrist okay. I understand that the job is necessary, but here's the thing about my imaginary friend."

Arnella rolled her eyes.

"Whenever you feel burdened and depressed, just talk to him. Tell him your stuff, whatever it is... My imaginary friend will make you feel better, just by talking to him. Ask him for peace about your situation, and I guarantee you will get it."

"He can't do anything about my kind of stuff." Arnella shuddered. "It's bad and getting out of control."

"He can do anything." Vanley kissed her on her forehead. "Promise me you'll try it."

Arnella wiggled her eyebrows. "Okay, Pastor, I promise."

"Don't break the promise," Vanley said gently.

"I won't. I'll talk to him like I would talk to Taj."

Vanley smiled. "So, Taj is your psychiatrist?"

"Yup, I like him. It's been a week. I've been venting about my childhood and other stuff."

Vanley held her hand in his and squeezed them. "Your childhood sucked, I know. How is school?"

"You ask me that every time we talk, you sound like a father." Arnella grinned, "I am going to stay up here. Uncle Ryan already threatened me. I think school is great, fantastic…couldn't be better."

Vanley chuckled. "Great. Fantastic. That's overkill."

"You asked for it." Arnella laughed. "So how are you and the secret girl that you told me you were pining over?"

Vanley tensed up. "I am twenty-five, an intern pastor. I don't pine."

"Hit a nerve?" Arnella asked gleefully.

"Yup," Vanley said, "It is not going too well."

"Why. She blind?" Arnella laughed. "You are not only good-looking but caring and kind, and you love Jesus. That should be an instant win for her."

"She's fifteen years older than I am," Vanley said softly.

"May-December in reverse?" Arnella chuckled. "Who is she?"

"Not telling you," Vanley said. "Not yet. Not when things are so shaky. If only I could get through to her."

"So when she is forty-five you will be just hitting thirty." Arnella scratched her chin. "Sounds like an awful gap."

Vanley snorted. "I don't care."

"Oh man, I couldn't do it," Arnella said. "When she was

in high school you were just being born...sounds sticky. Not too bad when it's the male who is older, but the other way around... I don't know."

Vanley shrugged. "She's the one I love."

"How do you know you love her?" Arnella asked. "What does this love feel like?"

Vanley looked at her. "You genuinely want to know, don't you?"

Arnella shrugged. "Yeah, I guess."

"I woke up one day and I realized that she wasn't just in my head. She was now occupying my heart. I just want to be with her and around her all the time without reservation and without reason."

Arnella nodded. "I see."

"It's that simple and that complicated." Vanley patted her leg. "I have to go. I have a meeting."

Arnella nodded. "It was nice talking to you."

Vanley kissed her on the cheek. "Remember to talk to Jesus, okay."

"I'll remember." Arnella watched him as he walked away and then waited for the morose feeling that had been swamping her to take over again, but it didn't come back.

She looked at her watch and headed for the Biology Lab.

*****

"Hey friend," Alric grinned at Arnella as she headed out of the class.

"Hi," Arnella smiled with him, suddenly feeling self-conscious around him. They watched one movie, had one long talk about nothing important, and all of a sudden she was jittery. She was an honest to goodness wuss of a girl. She was starting to act like Tracy; though from what she heard on Saturday night, Tracy was a Judas. Acted like a friend and then told Alric those whopping lies about her.

"I was wondering," Alric said, when she walked over to him, "do you want to participate in a fundraiser for the hospital?"

"I don't get it." Arnella shook her head. "What fundraiser?"

"Well, the Medical Student Association, of which I am a part, has a yearly fundraiser in December, around Christmas time. We throw a party, invite the big wigs in the community, charge them a hefty fee for tickets, and have an auction. Proceeds go to the hospital. Last year we bought an MRI machine."

Arnella started shaking her head, "I can't be auctioned. Sorry."

"Not you silly," Alric grinned, "a painting of yours."

"How do you know that my paintings are any good?" Arnella frowned.

Alric grinned. "I don't. Want to show them to me?"

"I am not sure," Arnella said, feeling unsettled again. "Listen Alric, about this friend thing..."

"No, you don't," Alric stood up from his desk. "I am your friend, I need to find you abhorrent, remember? You agreed. So we are friends you can't just unfriend me."

"Why not?" Arnella grunted. "I didn't know friendships had rule books."

"They do," Alric said, "and as a friend, I demand that you have lunch with me today."

Arnella frowned.

"And every Monday and Wednesday for that matter." Alric inclined his head. "I am free those periods."

Arnella opened her mouth to protest and then closed it with a snap.

"Trust me," Alric said, laughing at her mutinous expression,

"I make a great friend. You'll like me as a friend."

"Okay," Arnella threw her hand up in the air. "I doubt we have anything in common."

Alric grinned, "I am sure we do."

Chapter Eleven

Natasha called just as Arnella was preparing to go downstairs to paint. It was late in the evening, almost six. The evening had turned dark from about five-thirty.

"Sorry I took so long to call," Natasha said without preamble. "How are you doing?"

"Fine," Arnella said, "I thought you weren't going to call."

"Are you kidding?" Natasha asked. "What happened to you is serious, and your cousin, Kylie, is extremely worried about you."

Arnella cleared her throat. "I just want to forget the whole thing. I am sorry that I told her."

"It's a good thing that you told her," Natasha said stridently. "You suffered a terrible injustice. It was criminal. It was rape. Unfortunately, since you did not give a statement or do a rape kit, we are in a pickle. That video that you got could be potential evidence. I want to see it."

Arnella cleared her throat, "I got another one today, but I

didn't open it."

"Ah," Natasha murmured, "I heard you are living up at Deidra's place?"

"Yes," Arnella said reluctantly. Now that she was going to face the police about the whole thing, she felt as if she didn't want to anymore.

"I can be there in a few minutes," Natasha said, seeming to sense her reticence. "I'll bring my laptop." She hung up quickly, before Arnella could protest.

Arnella grabbed her laptop and sat with it on her lap, waiting for Natasha to arrive. She had resisted looking at the video because she was scared. The longer this whole thing went on, the more shaken up she was becoming. It was the uncertainty of not knowing what she did that day that was killing her. Sometimes she thought it was best not to remember, but at other times, she really wanted to know.

Natasha arrived half-an-hour later. When Arnella went to let her in, she realized that it was raining, and little flurries were swirling outside. Natasha was in a black windbreaker and black jeans.

"You look like a character from the Matrix." Arnella grinned. "Can you dodge bullets and do martial arts?"

Natasha smiled, "I have had to dodge several bullets. Martial arts? Yes. How are you?"

Arnella led her into the kitchen. "I don't know. I am seeing Taj. He tells me not to mask my feelings. I tend to internalize things. He said I should be honest. Now that you ask, I really don't know how I feel. Angry, sometimes frustrated. I don't sleep much anymore; I am constantly jittery."

She sat down in a chair, and Natasha sat beside her, taking out her laptop from her bag.

"That's understandable," Natasha said, "but I am going to have to ask you for specifics, okay? You have to tell me everything that you remember from the party." She pulled out her notebook.

Arnella sighed. "I went to Tracy's house."

"Tracy Carr?" Natasha asked jotting down the name. "How did you meet her?"

"She was a friend from high school," Arnella frowned. "I really can't remember how we started hanging out. She was the little rich girl that always came to school chauffer-driven. She had hip-length hair, which she flicked over her shoulders every chance she got. She had a superior attitude going on. All the girls loved to hate on her. I didn't think she was a bad person so we hung out. I guess this year would have been seven years of friendship."

"Past tense?" Natasha asked, pausing her writing.

"Yup. She likes a guy and thinks that he likes me, so she told him some dreadful lies about me."

"Ah," Natasha said, smoothly flipping the page of her notebook. "Did you confront her?"

"No," Arnella bit her lip. "I can't deal with that right now. I am trying to get through each day as it is. Losing Tracy as a friend is not very significant for me right now. To be honest, ever since she started Mount Faith, we have been on the outs."

"So she told these lies after the party?" Natasha asked.

"Yes. She is interested in Pastor Peterson's son, Alric."

"Nice guy. He plays the organ at church," Natasha said. "He does medicine, right?"

"Final year," Arnella said softly. "Then internship up here."

"So you like him?" Natasha grinned.

"I am not sure." Arnella started fidgeting. "Okay, I do a little. He is four years older than I am. We grew up in the same community. We are friends now, as of last week. He likes me."

"Was he at the party?" Natasha asked poised to write down his name.

"Yes, but just for a little while." Arnella frowned. "Tracy was dying for him to attend. She spent her whole freshman year following him around. I didn't see when he left the party."

"Who else was there that you know?" Natasha asked. "Take your time to remember. I am going to ask Tracy Carr for her guest list, but I need you to tell me who you knew."

Arnella nodded. "Well, there was Tracy, obviously, and then there was David Hudson. We went to high school together. He was nerdy. He received the prize for the highest ranked science student in the Caribbean Examination Council exams."

Natasha was jotting that down rapidly.

"Then there was Jeff Hill. He is another nerd. One time he and Tracy had a thing—senior year, high school. His parents own the Gimme A Bite restaurant chain. Jeff was a little guy all through high school and then suddenly, in fifth form, he became tall and cute."

Natasha grinned. "I knew a guy like that at my high school."

Arnella smiled. "There is always one, isn't there."

Natasha removed her jacket. "I am getting warm. You know, I predict that this will be the coldest winter in Mount Faith. It's just September and already I have to wear a jacket when I'm out. So, who else was there that you know?"

"Cory Livingston." Arnella shrugged. "He tried to chat me up from the moment I arrived at the party." She smirked. "He was always doing that to me in high school as well... following me around. I used to embarrass him, shoo him. It never worked. He was my adoring shadow."

"How many persons were there?" Natasha asked.

"Around thirty, I guess. There was the Mount Faith crowd, Tracy's new friends. They were friendly enough, but I didn't know them. I stayed in the pool most of the time. I didn't want to chat to the three guys that I actually knew from high school so I was feeling really bored. I was the only one who hadn't gone to sixth form and on to university, so I felt a bit left out of Tracy's life, you know."

Natasha nodded. "So you entered the party…stayed in the pool. What did you eat or drink?"

"I had a hot dog." Tracy had a caterer do the party. "I tried the hot dog and a slice of pizza then went to the bar and got a root beer. When it was finished, a guy came and refilled my root beer. A waiter."

"The bar?" Natasha asked, "Who was manning it?"

"A guy," Arnella shook her head, "I guess he worked with the catering company. He had on their uniform."

"How many beers did you drink?" Natasha flipped her notebook page again.

"About five, or six, but they were root beers." Arnella got up and stretched. "They were alcohol free. I don't drink alcohol. My Mom is an alcoholic, and my Dad died in a bar, so I vowed to stay away from that poison."

Natasha tapped her forehead with the pen. "Was Tracy serving alcohol?"

"No," Arnella shook her head. "It was an alcohol free party though David claimed he was drunk."

"Mmmh." Natasha scribbled something. "So you were in the pool and then you got out? Why?"

Arnella hung her head. She didn't want to face the reason why she had gotten out of the pool. She had been showing off for Alric, to be honest. She had wanted him to see her. She had wanted some reaction, so she had stretched in her little flimsy swimsuit. She was no better than Tracy had said.

A piece of her had found him interesting, just because Tracy had, probably.

She sighed, "I came out because I was showing off."

Natasha grinned. "You were?"

"Yes, it was about the time when Alric came on the scene. I wanted him to see my nipple ring and I wanted to give him a bad girl impression. You know, to confirm all the stuff that I know he had heard about me. The people in my community thrived on rumors and I was their favorite topic."

"And then what happened?" Natasha was watching her closely.

"Then David came up to me and put his arm around me. He is taller than me you know; my head probably reaches his chin. He said, 'Nella, we would like to propose a toast to maturity, long life, and success,' or something like that. He handed me a cup, one of those red plastic ones, then Cory and Jeff came by, grinning."

I clicked my cup with theirs then drank the root beer. It tasted slightly off but I guzzled it down. I then remember David moving up close to my face and asking me if I felt okay.

Then Jeff said something about me looking like a short supermodel and then I laughed. Like an idiot."

Arnella hissed her teeth. "I laughed. Then the next thing I know everything started to look fuzzy and I mumbled that I was going to have to sit down, maybe change into my regular clothes. I had gotten fed up of the party. I think it was David, or Jeff who held my hand and said he'd help me to the changing room. Next thing I knew it was morning and I was in the Carr's guest room."

Natasha nodded. "Let me see the video."

Arnella glanced at her computer uncertainly. "I don't want to see it really. I can't bear to."

"That's okay," Natasha said, "I'll watch it."

Arnella pointed to the two emails and watched as Natasha clicked on the video links.

Natasha's expressions didn't change much during the videos. When she finally looked up at Arnella she said slowly. "This was carefully edited."

"The second video?" Arnella asked anxiously.

"Yes, both of them. It actually looks as if you were aware of what was going on." Natasha drummed her pen on the table. "Who were you waving to in the opening scene of the first video?"

Arnella sighed. "Alric. He was looking around for Tracy and I yelled something to him."

"They also showed you stretching seductively." Natasha shook her head. "I presume that was also when you were showing off for Alric?"

Arnella ran her fingers through her hair in frustration. "It looks bad, doesn't it?"

"Did you see anyone around with a video camera while you were waving?" Natasha was also looking confused.

"No. No." Arnella shook her head vehemently. "To the right of the pool, there were only people dancing and that seems to be the angle of the video. I caused this, didn't I? If I wasn't so provocatively dressed, I wouldn't have been in this situation."

Natasha frowned. "This video is not your fault. It is not time to panic yet. The video footage is very damning, yes. I am not going to lie. In the first clip, you look happy. The videographer zoomed in on your tongue ring. You then came out of the pool and stretched elegantly like you knew you were being watched. Then there is a clip with you in a room, passionately kissing a guy. Only the side of his face is visible. Then there is a clip where they are taking off your clothes but only your face is visible, then there is one with your head, back, and spine arched with one guy, whose face is obscured, licking your body. You looked like you were enjoying it."

Arnella squeezed her eyes shut. "I don't remember any of that. I really don't remember the pool room part, except for some fuzzy pieces."

"Who knows this email address?" Natasha asked.

"I use it for everything." Arnella said despairingly. "I don't know who knows. It is no secret."

"How long have you had it?" Natasha had her pen poised above the paper.

"Since I was sixteen, nearly five years ago. That's why it's called Arnella16." Arnella scrunched up her face. "This doesn't look good, does it? Be honest with me."

Natasha shook her head. "It doesn't. If I didn't hear your side of the story and know that you are genuinely hurting over this video, I'd say you were posing for it and that you wanted this. Unfortunately, there is no evidence that there was a crime committed here unless somebody at the party can verify that they saw someone put whatever drug was used into your cup. Even then, a clever lawyer can have the case dismissed in a jiffy. This video is damning, but as yet, there is no blackmail or anything to prove that this is a crime."

Tears came to Arnella's eyes and she blinked them back. "All I did was go to a lousy party. I admit that I could have turned down the sex appeal a bit more, well a huge chunk more. I don't want these videos to get out. I didn't consent to it. Can't you do something about that?"

Natasha patted her on her hand. "There are still some things we can do."

"Like what?" Arnella sniffed.

"I could ask my friend, Miles, from the cyber crime unit to trace the email address of whoever sent this thing. She looked at the address again. Both videos were sent from the EasterBunny@mail.com. That would save us loads of trouble of going to investigate on our own. The only problem is this kind of information will take weeks to get because there is some red tape involved. Email addresses are usually private and protected closely by the companies who issue them. In the meantime, I am going to check out David, Cory, and Jeff and find out exactly who took this video of you and whether there are any copies and whether any of them sent the emails."

Arnella sighed, a huge juddering motion that did nothing to loosen the panic in her mind.

"Hang in there," Natasha said softly. "I have no pacifying words to tell you, but I know how this must feel. If I can find out who used this date rape drug on you, I will personally make sure that they serve some time behind bars. This is abhorrent and criminal."

Chapter Twelve

It was shaping up to be an extremely wet September. It had been two days since Arnella had her interview with Natasha, and she was finding it hard not to blame herself for her current misfortune. In her session with Taj, he had told her that she was a victim and wasn't to be blamed, but she couldn't help but playing what-if-games in her head.

What if she hadn't worn that revealing bikini? What if she hadn't tried to show off for Alric? What if she wasn't trying to be the life of the party? She would have been okay now. She wouldn't have been sexually assaulted and had a video of her in the hands of grimy pervs. God forbid that it starts floating around in cyberspace.

Arnella stepped into the Business Center. She had to eat some lunch. Her appetite had been playing hide and seek with her. She looked around the courtyard. Students were seated in little pockets around the indoor palm trees, talking and laughing. They looked so carefree and untouched by melancholy. That's exactly how she pictured that university students should look anyway, not burdened down with a million and one problems.

Then she saw a head moving up and down in laughter and she realized that it was Cory Livingston. *One of the criminals,* she thought snarkily. He was in a green shirt and was sitting with a group of his friends. One girl had her hand around his neck in a possessive manner.

So he found something funny, she thought resentfully. He could laugh and carry on with his life while she was miserable. She clenched her fists in anger. She wanted to do to Cory the same thing that she did to David, but she couldn't. Not here. Not now. She would surely be arrested for assault, and that would not make her life any easier. She wondered if Natasha had interviewed them yet. Then she thought not. He wouldn't be there, acting all carefree, if he knew that she had reported him to the police.

She walked to the cafeteria section feeling anger and guilt erupting inside her. Then she stopped at the doorway. Maybe she wasn't hungry after all. She had no appetite and she didn't want to run into Cory because she would attack him in anger, and it would not be pretty. She would surely overreact; she knew it.

She was turning around to leave the cafe area when she saw Alric turning around from the counter with a tray in hand.

"Hey," he called to her. "What's going on?"

Arnella smiled half-heartedly. "Nothing much."

There was a girl standing beside him. She was in a white lab coat. Her hair was caught up in a high ponytail, and she had on braces. She had slanted eyes that indicated some kind of Asian descent. She grinned when she saw Arnella.

"Want to have lunch with us?" Alric asked her.

Arnella shook her head.

"Come on," the girl said. "I want to have lunch with a non-medical."

"A non-medical?" Arnella asked.

"Yup, someone who is not into medicine and isn't likely to talk about it. I want to hear about what is going on in regular school."

"This is Kim Lee," Alric said to Arnella. "She is going to be the youngest graduate from med school in recent history."

"Uh," Kim said, "we are going to go sit over there. Go get something to eat and come join us."

Arnella made a face. "Not hungry. I'll just come join you."

They headed to the other side of the courtyard to where Cory was. Arnella sat with her back toward him, across from Kim and Alric.

Alric had a worried expression on his face. "I don't understand. You aren't eating again."

Kim's eyes perked up. "Are you sick? Should we diagnose her?"

Alric glanced at Kim. "Okay, shoot."

"Well," Kim looked at Arnella assessingly. "She looks a bit underweight to me. I would guess anorexia or maybe bulimia."

"But there are no telltale signs around her lips." Alric said, looking at Arnella. "They look pink and soft, not cracked at all and..."

"Can we change the subject?" Arnella said quickly, "I am neither bulimic nor anorexic, and I thought you said you wanted to talk to a non-medical."

Kim laughed. "I know right. It always comes back to medicine for me. I hope you aren't sick though and all this concern is just from an overly sensitive med school boyfriend."

"He's not my boyfriend," Arnella said quickly.

Kim laughed and looked at Alric's crestfallen expression. "He'd like to be though."

Arnella drummed her fingers on the table impatiently. If she were really honest, she'd like to be his girlfriend. Somewhere along the line, her perspective on Alric had shifted. She had gone from seeing him as a stuck up snob to seeing him as a guy she would have loved to date, but he wouldn't want to be her boyfriend if he knew what she was facing now. Alric didn't seem as if he would want somebody like her. He was better off with Tracy's type: circumspect in all her ways, ambitious, good family background.

She sighed involuntarily. Alric looked up from his food, frowning. Kim looked at Arnella at the same time. "So tell me about life outside of the medical building."

Arnella looked away from Alric. "I have no idea. I am here under duress so I just go to class and then home to work on my paintings."

"Interesting," Kim said, "I hear a lot of people say they are forced by their parents to come here. Not me, I couldn't wait to get out of high school."

"Which she did when she was just fourteen," Alric said admiringly. "Kim here is a genius."

"But," Kim said, "I am hopelessly underdeveloped socially. Just this morning I heard some girls talking to each other about a sex tape going around. I heard it had something to do with the president. If you ask me, I am not interested in seeing the president of this university in a lewd position."

Arnella felt her blood run cold. Her mouth fell open and she struggled to breathe. Sex tape. It must be the one with her!

"That's only a rumor," Alric said, "and since I have become friends with Arnella, I am counseling myself to stop listening to rumors. These things are whack. No truth to them. Right Arnella?"

Arnella wanted to run from the building, all the way down the hill to the plains of Santa Cruz and into her house, and lock the door and never talk to anyone again. "Right," she answered Alric faintly. "I think I am coming down with something."

Kim raised her eyebrows. "I hope it's not the flu. I can't afford to catch anything now."

Arnella shook her head. "I hope not; gotta run."

She got up and headed to the courtyard exit. She hadn't even realized that Alric was at her heels; he grabbed her hand and spun her around when they were away from the Business Center.

"What's wrong?"

Arnella's eyes watered. "Nothing." She cleared her throat. "Nothing."

Alric nodded. "I don't believe you. You were clearly upset when you heard about a sex tape involving your uncle. Don't worry about it; they have rumors flying around the campus all the time."

"They do?" Arnella asked calming down enough to think about it. Maybe she had overreacted because the words sex tape was a hot button issue for her. Maybe there really was a coincidental rumor about a tape going around. She breathed out. She was super sensitive these days.

"Yup." Alric grinned. "There was a time when there was this rumor going around that the old president was murdered by his gay lover. They even said your uncle did it."

Arnella smiled. "I heard that one."

"Then there was this rumor that Micah was the rapist around campus a couple of years ago. Of course, that proved to be untrue and then there was a rumor that your cousin

Adrian was hiding Cathy from that druggist guy. What's his name again? Nanjo."

Arnella inhaled and then exhaled in a huff. "Okay. I see where this is going; my family is a target for the rumor mill."

"You know I never knew that you felt this way about rumors," Alric said ruefully, "You always seemed so unaffected by them. Listen, Arnella," he said, holding her hand, "I am sorry I listened to all the crap I heard about you and believed them."

Arnella chuckled. "Does this mean that you don't think I am morally bankrupt anymore?"

Alric frowned. "I decided to forget what I saw and judge you on what I know now. Okay?"

"'Kay." Arnella felt a raindrop land on her forehead, and she looked up at the sky. "Another downpour is coming. What are you going to do now?"

Alric grinned a lopsided grin that showed off his left dimple. "I am going to interpret that question as you wanting to spend time with me. As a matter of fact, I planned to go to my apartment and continue studying for the infamous Multiple Mini Interview."

"What's that?" Arnella asked, suddenly not wanting to be alone and wanting to hang with him a bit longer.

"That's when they ask you questions based on your whole medical career in a circuit interview setting. You can't graduate med school without this dreaded interview cycle."

"So you will be finished this year?"

"Yes," Alric nodded, "from med school. Then it's internship at the Medical Center and then three years residency. By that time, I'll be twenty-seven. Do you think you can handle having an intern doctor friend for three years?"

The rain started pouring down in earnest, but Arnella couldn't move. Was he asking her to be his girlfriend? Was this his backhanded way of asking?

They stared at each other while the rain came down harder. Little rivulets of water were winding their way down his smooth nutmeg skin to his lips. Arnella watched them fascinatedly then finally shook her head. "Of course. I'll be your friend, if that's what you want."

Alric smiled slowly. "That's a start. You're wet."

"So are you," Arnella said shyly.

"Want to come to my apartment and dry off?" Alric asked.

Arnella thought about it for so long that Alric folded his arms and shook his head, "I promise; I will behave myself."

Arnella wondered if she could trust him. She had just come from a situation where she was finding it difficult to trust men. She finally nodded.

"Good," Alric said playfully, "because I am getting soaked here."

The air felt freezing as they walked together toward the Blue Palm Apartments.

"I have always wanted to do this," Arnella said, laughing up at Alric. "I have never in my whole life walked in the rain before, not caring about my hair or if I step into puddles... just walking."

Alric deliberately stepped in a puddle and said, "Stepping in puddles is the best way to do this."

Arnella giggled and stepped in one too. "This is liberating."

Alric laughed. "I have never done this either, so it's a first for us."

Arnella nodded brushing off the dark cloud that hung over her head when he said that. There was no space for dark clouds here. She thought ironically, looking up at the gray skies. She pushed out her tongue and tried to catch raindrops.

Alric laughed and did the same.

*****

Tracy had just driven home from her Business Law class, the last class of the day. She had two classes on Friday morning and then she had the weekend free. It was going to be a wet weekend. She wished she had someone to spend the weekend with, not just someone, but Alric.

She smiled to herself and turned into the Blue Palm Apartment parking lot. Several times she had gone to visit Alric and knocked on his door, but there was no response. At least he was working hard and not feeling concerned for Arnella, she thought resentfully. She had had to nip that softening of his attitude toward Arnella in the bud. Her methods were not right, but she was learning to live with it. She hoped that he did not tell Arnella what she told him, but from the disgust he show toward her the last time, she seriously doubted that he would be telling Arnella anything.

She got out of the car, struggling with her flimsy umbrella and her bag of books. She headed for Block C then thought about going to Block F instead, where Alric lived. She had never tried knocking on his door at three in the evening. She smiled to herself.

She had no idea what the inside of his apartment looked like, but she knew there was a standard kitchenette, living room, bedroom, and bathroom. Students usually gave it their own touch, as she did hers with her pink and white accessories. Maybe she could invite herself to decorate for him. She walked briskly to Block D, the rain was pouring down harder, and even though she was walking on the corridor, it was blowing in her direction.

She counted the numbers as she walked by. Alric was on F3. She knocked on the door briskly, looking around; not wanting anybody to see that she was once again loitering outside his door. She was surprised when she heard movement in the apartment and a pleased smile stretched across her lips when the door opened slowly. Her smile quickly fell when Arnella, her hair damp and a towel in one hand, opened the door. She was dressed in one of Alric's sweatshirts, which reached her almost to her knees. Arnella smirked when she saw Tracy.

Tracy was dumbstruck. She could not formulate a word when she saw her.

Arnella kept on rubbing her hair. "Yes?" she enquired snarkily.

"I came to see Alric," Tracy said, swallowing the bile that was rising to her throat.

Arnella nodded. "He is in the shower. We just got in."

Tracy nodded jerkily. "So are you two a couple now?"

Arnella stopped rubbing her hair and smiled. "Would it kill you to know? You two-faced Judas."

"Why are you calling me that?" Tracy asked innocently.

"You told Alric that I had a test called an Arnella test. What was with that?"

Tracy clutched her book bag even tighter as she realized that she was caught in a lie. She didn't even know where to look. She couldn't deny it now when Alric was right inside the apartment.

"I am sorry; I was jealous, don't know what came over me," she said quickly and insincerely.

"Jealous of what?" Arnella asked incredulously.

"Alric likes you." Tracy hissed, "and he's the one guy that I have ever really liked. You just had to snatch him away, didn't you?"

Arnella laughed, "Tracy when have I ever snatched anybody away from you? Are you hallucinating?"

A fiery anger gripped Tracy's chest. "You always do it with every single guy. You are a monster. A whoring monster."

She walked away from Arnella in a huff and headed to Block C. She didn't even care if the rain was blowing on her. She headed to her apartment slammed the door and slumped on it, an ache in her chest. She listened vaguely to the rain slapping the pavement outside and crawled toward her phone.

She dialed her house number. It was three in the afternoon; she didn't expect anybody to be home but she just wanted to talk to sympathetic listeners. Her mother and father were just that, well more her father because he hated Arnella. She had to admit that that was her fault because she had complained about Arnella to him for years.

Her father picked up on the third ring.

"Dad," Tracy said chokily. "What are you doing home?"

"Can you believe I have the flu?" he coughed for a spate. "Why are you sounding so sad?"

"It's Arnella again," Tracy wailed. "She is seeing Alric, the guy I like. I don't know what's the matter with her. She just can't see me liking someone without stealing them."

Her father grunted. "I hope you are still not having a friendship with her? She's really something else, isn't she?"

"Yes," Tracy said mournfully. "I hate her."

Her father grunted. "There are just some people you have to avoid, Tracy hun. Arnella is one of them. Don't let her know what is going on in your life. Ignore her. Soon you'll move on with your career. She'll still be mediocre. One day she'll get ugly and washed up, and you'll wonder what you were so bothered about. She'll be nothing and you'll be something."

Tracy smiled. "Thanks Dad. I can always depend on you to set me straight."

"Don't mention it," her father sneezed. "By the way, I am coming to the Medical Association Ball in December...just bought two tickets. Want to be my date? Your mother has a conference the same week and can't attend."

"Yes. Sure," Tracy said. That's Alric's school club; he'd definitely be there. Maybe if she dressed to the nines and looked really good, she could show him what he was missing by being with Arnella.

*****

"Who was that?" Alric came out of the bathroom dressed in jeans and t-shirt. He smelled really good and fresh with the remnants of a lemony scent.

"That was Tracy," Arnella said grinning. "She called me a whoring monster."

Alric looked at her diminutive figure in his sweatshirt and shook his head. "That's not even funny, Arnella. "

"It is," Arnella said. "I can't believe she told you that there was some sort of Arnella test. Now she is probably back in her apartment, crying her eyes out. I find that funny."

Alric sat in his overstuffed green chair and frowned at her, "I find your sexual life troubling."

"Why?" Arnella said, sitting across from him in a huff. "It has nothing to do with you."

"It does Arnella," Alric said exasperated. "I know you are sexually experienced, I understand that. I just don't like to think about it, you know. I get really angry when I think about it. Call me old-fashioned."

Arnella looked down at her hand, "I don't want to talk about this. What happened to us being only friends?"

Alric nodded and grabbed up one of his textbooks. "Okay. We are just friends. I don't care how many men you sleep with, or where you go, or what you do."

He leafed through one of the textbooks angrily, and Arnella

looked over at his stack of books and DVD collection under his television.

"How many have you slept with?" Alric asked quietly.

Arnella looked at him, "I thought you were studying."

"I need to know," Alric said. "Yes, I know it is deeply uncool to ask, but I wonder and sometimes I do it at the most inappropriate times, and I get jealous of all those faceless guys that have been trampling in and out of your life."

Arnella sighed and got up. "I don't want to talk about this. Not with you. Not now."

Alric pursed his lips and then looked down into his book. "Okay."

"What about your sex life?" Arnella asked gruffly. "Since you are so fascinated with mine, tell me about yours."

Alric looked up from his book slowly. "My sex life is pretty simple and straightforward. I have not had sex yet. Still resisting peer pressure and societal pressure to be some sort of stud."

For some reason, that deflated Arnella and she leaned back in the couch feeling like a dirty specimen.

"That's admirable," she whispered, "waiting for the right girl."

Alric inclined his head and looked at her intently. "I don't want admiration. I don't even want to like you."

"I don't want to like you either," Arnella said brashly. "Bad boys are much more appealing. You are as straight as an arrow. You cross all your t's and dot all your i's. You are a good guy. I don't want you to like me. I might jinx you, turn you into a bad person."

Alric put aside his book and folded his arm. "You can't jinx me, and you are not a bad person. I am surprised your psychiatrist hasn't addressed that problem of yours yet."

"What problem?" Arnella snarled.

"The one where you think you are the worst person in the world, an untouchable." Alric laughed. "You are not, you know, and you don't have to try to prove that to me. You have some redeeming qualities that I like."

"What are some of those redeeming qualities that you see in me?" Arnella asked softly.

Alric smiled. "You act tough but you are a softie. You actually cried when we dissected that frog in the lab."

"Something was in my eye," Arnella said. "Allergies. That's it. I had allergies. I am allergic to dead frogs."

"You feel deeply," Alric said softly "about everything. You are passionate and opinionated and independent and talented."

Arnella shivered uncomfortably.

"And that's what I have found out in a month. I am still trying to unravel the mystery of Arnella though," Alric said, picking up his book again. "Want to ask me some practice questions and hear my deeply intelligent answers?"

Arnella rolled her eyes. "Sure."

*****

As usual, Arnella couldn't sleep. She had turned into an insomniac. She found it hard to settle her mind after she had dug up her past with Taj. All of her childhood angst and pain came roaring back afresh.

She glanced at the clock. It was six o' clock in the morning. Instead of running downstairs to paint before her class, she had taken to talking to Jesus, as Vanley had made her promise.

She told Him about her day, and she told Him what she wanted to do and asked for His help. It usually made her feel better. She had also taken to reading snippets of the Bible.

Alric had been the one to encourage her to read it. "There are no perfect people in there," he had told her seriously after one of their long talks. "Trust me, you'll find company. The one thing the Bible characters had in common is that they had a God who loved them, who went out of his way to save them, just like he is doing for you and I. He loves you Arnella."

She pushed herself out of bed and got on her knees. God loved her. The more she thought about it the more special she felt. She was not used to feeling special for anybody. She also felt sorry now that she had mocked Vanley and called Jesus his imaginary friend. He was not imaginary in the least. Whenever she tentatively asked him for peace about her situation, she really did feel it. She couldn't explain how that worked, but it did.

Her phone chirped on the bedside table and she picked it up slowly.

"Arnella Bancroft." It was her uncle. "I can't even process this madness that Kylie told me last week. You were raped and videotaped by boys attending this institution, and nothing is being done about it."

"Hello to you too Uncle Ryan," Arnella said, flinching at every word he spoke. "Glad to hear that you are back from your trip."

"And to think that you did not want to tell anybody!" Bancroft bellowed over the phone. "My office, ten o'clock today, Arnella!"

He hung up the phone in her ears in an angry huff.

It was two weeks and Arnella hadn't heard from Natasha. She had honestly thought that Natasha had forgotten her, but when she walked into her uncle's office at ten o'clock, there was Natasha and another guy sitting beside her. Jackie Beecher, the school's lawyer and Kylie's chief nemesis was there as well.

"Have a seat," her uncle said to her after the brief pleasantries were exchanged. The guy who was sitting with Natasha was a detective too. His name was Tony Beaker. That much she learnt before her uncle, like a bulldozer, started the conversation.

"I spoke to the Assistant Supe Coley last night and heard that you were looking into this case," he said to Natasha briskly.

"Yes," Natasha said. "I interviewed the guys involved."

She looked at Arnella apologetically. "They all said it had been Arnella's idea that they do a video at the party. They also said that they dumped the video. Apparently, Cory was the videographer. David had penetrative sex with her and Jeff oral sex.

According to Cory, they ran out of time because they were almost caught. They all denied giving her a drug."

Natasha shrugged. "I am sorry Arnella; there is nothing we can legally do about the situation now."

Ryan Bancroft thumped the desk. "What about a search warrant to find out if one of those cretins had the date rape drug on them?"

Natasha shook her head. "There is no evidence to get a warrant. Unfortunately, Arnella did not do a rape kit or report the rape to the police in time. This whole thing is now a matter of he said she said."

"I was not even sure if there had been a rape at the time," Arnella said weakly. "The first thing I did was bathe. I can't even remember what really happened and I refuse to watch anymore of those videos."

"About the videos," Natasha said, "I have my friend Miles in the cyber crime unit looking into it. He said we'd get results from the email company in a month or so."

"How can I expel those brutes?" Ryan turned to Jackie, who had been silent while Natasha spoke.

"Well," Jackie said, "you can't. Not without legal reason. They could sue the school for wrongful dismissal. It would be too messy and the publicity would be awful."

Bancroft sighed. "And that video. Where did the guys dump the copy?"

Natasha shrugged. "Cory explained that he took the SD card and dumped it in the garbage can at the party, before they left. According to him they panicked that anyone would see them on it so they dropped it in the garbage."

"He sounds like he's lying," Jackie said cynically. "Why go through all the effort of taping a sex scene and then dump it."

"I think we have a greater chance of finding out who is the culprit if we track that email address," Natasha said.

"You prefer to wait to find out an email address before doing good old detective work?" Jackie asked incredulously.

Natasha tensed her mouth. "We have to wait on the email service provider to give us information about the account holder of the email address. That can take a while but we'll have the exact location of whoever is sending the mail. It's much easier that way. If the person shares it online or sells it, then Arnella can sue for invasion of privacy."

Jackie sneered. "I think you are not doing your job as efficiently as you could."

"Ladies, ladies," Bancroft said snappily, before Natasha could retort. "I know you two have a personal issue, but please, let's not bring this into the current matter. My niece has been wronged. Is there anyway to make this legally right?"

Both Natasha and Jackie shook their heads.

Tony spoke up. He was all but ignored in the room. "Are

you sure that the guys dumped the storage device? It's a reusable card, why dump it?"

"Explain," Bancroft said, scratching his chin.

"Some video cameras use a little card, called a SD card, to store recorded images and videos. That is not something you just take out and dump. Maybe they are lying. Maybe they didn't dump it and are tormenting Arnella with the video."

Natasha shrugged. "Short of putting them in a torture chamber and wringing a confession out of them, I don't know how you can tell if their story is straight. Obviously, they all came together and rehearsed their side of the story."

"What about the part where somebody spooked them? Didn't they say they thought they were going to be caught or something? Who is that person? Maybe they are the ones with the video?"

Natasha nodded. "That's a possibility. We'll find out when that email address is traced."

"The really bad part about all of this is that some date rape drugs are legally dispensed at pharmacies," Jackie said, sighing. "We can't get them on illegally possessing drugs either."

"So that's it?" Bancroft said "That's all there is to this sordid mess?"

"I hope not," Natasha said feelingly. "I really hate the injustice of this whole matter."

Arnella cleared her throat. She more than hated it. She couldn't recall feeling so many negative emotions in the space of one month.

The meeting continued a little longer, then her uncle asked her to stay back. She watched as the others walked through the door then looked at her uncle, wide-eyed.

"Please don't yell at me for not telling you. I just didn't know how to handle the whole thing."

Bancroft sighed heavily, "I can't imagine how this is affecting you. I heard that you are getting some help though."

Arnella nodded. "I am."

"That's good." Bancroft cleared his throat. "Things like this can have a long running effect on a woman's life and future relationships."

"I am coping." Arnella twisted her fingers, her voice breaking. "I am actually talking to a guy."

She wasn't used to having heart-to-heart talks with her uncle, but being honest with her feelings was really turning her into a wuss. She was tearing up over the least little thing.

"Oh dear." Bancroft came around to her side of the desk and patted her shoulders.

"I am sure this whole thing will look better some day. Maybe far in the future, hang tight kid. Hang tight."

Arnella sniffed. "Thanks Uncle Ryan. I have class now."

He nodded and watched her go, though his brow was furrowed and he had a worried look on his face.

Chapter Thirteen

Arnella woke up on the first day of October unexpectedly happy. Maybe it was the fact that she had finally gotten a full night's sleep. She even dressed in a bright yellow top and a pair of paint-splatter-free jeans. She wanted to match the day, which was sunshiney with the hint of a fresh breeze. The rural town of Mount Faith suddenly felt like home to her. Going to school was not all bad after all.

She drove down toward Mount Faith and was fortunate to hear the song "I Can See Clearly Now That The Rain Is Gone." She was even humming to the refrain "it's gonna be a bright, bright sunshiny day." She was still humming when she entered her computer class and gave Saidie a breezy good morning. They had gotten to know each other over the course of the semester.

Saidie found computers to be a troubling necessity and needed help with everything. Arnella was quite happy to help her. Saidie was a primary school teacher and a motherly figure type who was nearing retirement age but was determined to get her first degree in education. "Maybe I can use it with my grandkids," she joked to Arnella.

This morning, Saidie was looking downcast when Arnella sat beside her.

"Arnella," Saidie whispered as soon as she sat down, "don't take this the wrong way but have you seen the Mount Faith Gossip."

She drew it out of her bag cautiously, looking at Arnella sympathetically. "Some kids are handing them out in the Business Center courtyard. I usually don't read these kind of things but..."

Arnella laughed. "Why are you so solemn?"

Saidie pointed to the headlines: "The President's Niece Is A Slut, by Anonymous."

Arnella gasped. "What?"

"Read it," Saidie said, still in that solemn tone of hers.

Arnella inhaled several times before her breathing could get back to normal.

The president of Mount Faith can't seem to keep his family in check. His niece, Arnella Bancroft, is the star in what appears to be an erotic video. There is no mistaking that it's her in the very juicy video that we have gotten our hands on. We rate it five stars for being hot. Why is she attending Mount Faith again? Surely, she does not need higher education when she has such a banging body, which she can use ably. Seeing is believing. Take our word for it.

"No, no, no," Arnella said shaking her head frantically. "No!"

Saidie nodded. "I know it's not true. I grabbed some of them from the guy who was handing them out and beat him with it."

Arnella groaned and banged her head on the computer

screen. "I was having a good day. I mean, I woke up this morning, it was all bright and sunshiny…"

"Forget about it." Saidie patted her back. "It will blow over. I don't know why people like this kind of fabricated gossip."

Arnella looked around the lab. There were usually thirty of them in the class. She suddenly realized that most eyes were on her. Some people were being subtle about it but others were staring at her and whispering.

"I have to go," she said to Saidie, mournfully.

"Don't you dare move," Saidie said sternly. "You will act as if this does not bother you. Okay?"

"But," Arnella said lowly, "there is a video. The guys who did it drugged me. I can't handle this Saidie."

"Yes, you can," Saidie said. "So why aren't they in prison rotting now?"

"It's a long story," Arnella whispered back. "I'll tell you at another time."

Saidie nodded, her neatly combed partly gray hair bobbing up and down. "I will curse anyone who dares to mention it in my presence."

"Oh thank you, Saidie," Arnella said, feeling a tingling of warmth toward her friend.

The teacher stepped into the class and she looked around. Spotting Arnella, her eyes widened.

Arnella groaned; obviously she had heard the rumor as well. She turned on her computer and gritted her teeth. She had been weathering rumors for years but that was when she knew they were untrue. Now she was in uncharted waters.

She went into her email and saw another mail from EasterBunny@mail.com. She clicked on it, there was no video attached. She exhaled deeply, her fingers trembling. There was a message though; it was all in caps. "EXPOSE

THE BAD GIRL."

Arnella shuddered. She could barely go through class. Like the first time she had gotten one of the vidoes, she was feeling unaccountably jittery and on edge. When she exited class with Saidie beside her like a sentinel, she found Kylie and Gareth at the door.

"We were waiting for your class to be over," Kylie said hugging her. "Do you have any idea who could be doing this?" She clutched a sheet of the Gossip Newsletter in her hand.

"I asked Jackie to look into it," Gareth said reassuringly. "Something similar happened to me, but that was the school's official newspaper. I don't know who does this paper."

Arnella inhaled. "I am fine. I have Bio Lab now. I am just going to go and then head home."

Kylie stomped her foot, "I feel so angry about this."

"I know, me too." Arnella said feeling deflated. "I have to go."

They watched her as she slumped her shoulders and walked through the building. She wasn't going to go to Bio Lab though she had told them that. That was Alric's class. She couldn't bear to see the look on his face when he heard this latest rumor. She headed to her car. She was going to go home, to the basement. With her art, she could forget about school, and rumors.

*****

Alric had done one of those all nighters in the medical library for a group assignment. He had just gotten home and showered. He had Biology lab class now and the only reason he was looking forward to it was because he would see Arnella. He yawned and turned on his computer screen.

He usually checked his mail on a Wednesday to see what was new. He clicked on one that read, "Arnella as you've never seen her."

He did all of this absently while he sipped on some herbal tea. It was a video of Tracy's party. His spine stiffened as he watched the video play out. He hit pause before it got raunchier. He sat down abruptly on the chair around his desk, splashing some of the tea on the floor. He put it down gingerly on his desk and rubbed his hand over his face.

A sex tape? He felt a ringing in his ears. He had seen her that day with those guys but didn't suspect that she had been doing a sex tape. He felt the tea roiling in his stomach and he felt like throwing up. He clenched and unclenched his fist in anger. Didn't he know that getting involved with Arnella would involve this kind of thing?

He looked at his screen again and deleted the mail in disgust. His curiosity though had him searching back in his trash to see who had sent it. EasterBunny@mail.com

He shook his head. He was going to have a hard time staring at Arnella today. He didn't even know if he could talk to her again. He felt the same kind of anger and jealousy that he had felt at the same party when he saw her go off with those guys, except now he had gotten to know her and he felt like strangling her in rage.

He inhaled and exhaled, grabbed his knapsack and headed for his car. When he reached the class Arnella wasn't there. The class was feverishly excited though.

"Have you heard about the president's niece, Arnella?" One guy asked him waving a newsletter. "She's a porn star. How cool is that? I am going to school with a porn star."

Alric felt a buzzing in his ear when the pimply-faced guy guffawed and hit the desk. "Stop it," he growled. "No mention of pornography now, please. It's class time."

He had just stopped himself from defending Arnella, how stupid was he? He had partially seen that video. He handed out the papers, a heavy weight settling on his heart. He felt heart broken in a way that was puzzling. He was not only feeling like a jackass for believing that Arnella was a good person who was heavily misunderstood, but he was feeling an ounce of sympathy for her; unless, of course, she was really a porn star.

He slapped the pile of activities that he had on his desk with unnecessary force. "Work time. Today we are looking at bones."

*****

Bancroft was trodding around his office. He loosened his tie and growled to Security Chief Green and Jackie Beecher, who he had called as soon as he got wind of the latest gossip. "Get the slimeballs who wrote The Gossip."

Jackie tapped her pen on the table. "Now, Dr. Bancroft. There is a video; Arnella stars in it."

"Stars?" Ryan bellowed. "She was exploited! Here is what is going to happen:" the veins at the side of his head were throbbing. "I am going to expel those guys who were in the video, all three of them! Then, I am going to expel everyone who writes for The Gossip. How is that for justice? Then I am going to sue all of them for spreading these vicious lies!"

His phone rang and he picked it up. It was Kylie. He had sent her to follow Arnella. "Taj is here with her," Kylie said. "She's threatening to never leave the basement."

Bancroft grunted. "Make sure she is not alone. I don't want her to hurt herself."

He hung up the phone with Kylie and tapped his fingers on the desk.

Chief Green cleared his throat, "Dr. Bancroft, there is a little thing called freedom of speech."

"Not on this campus." Bancroft growled. "Not when this freedom is causing undue pain."

Jackie sighed, "Once Chief Green finds out who the persons are who wrote the paper, I can impress upon them the fact that there was a crime committed, and that it's under investigation... have them do a retraction. Threaten them with legal action that sort of thing. Scare them to thy kingdom come. The problem with this sort of thing though, is that the rumor is already rife. It is the hottest topic on campus. Pretty soon it will be the hottest topic in the community, then the rest of Jamaica, and with the Internet, the world."

Bancroft's phone rang again. It was Natasha. "Dr. Bancroft, I found out who the guys are who are behind the paper, they are Delano Davis and Kingsley Huffman. Both of them were sent the video by EasterBunny and were told to spread the word. They are sophomores in the English Department. They do this paper every Wednesday."

"Thanks," Bancroft said gruffly. "How is the tracking of the video coming on?"

"My contact at the Cybercrimes Unit is on top of it," Natasha said.

Bancroft hung up the phone and looked at Jackie. "I want them scared. Real scared. Natasha said they do the paper every Wednesday. They had better write a retraction this Thursday."

Jackie nodded and got up. "I am on it right now. Is there anything else?"

"Yes, prepare for a law suit from the families of those three boys." Bancroft growled, "because they are out of here, lawsuit or not."

He nodded to Chief Green. "Get those criminals to my

office as soon as possible."

Chief Green stood up as well "Okay, Sir. Are you going to do what we discussed?"

"Yes," Bancroft said, "as soon as they get here."

Bancroft paced around until his secretary called and announced that there were three gentlemen to see him.

"Gentlemen?" He snorted. "Send the brutes in!" he snarled over the phone. He was fit to burst with anger.

When he saw the three boys trooping into his office he wrestled with his emotions and adopted a calmer stance. They were even smiling with him, uncertainly.

"Sit down." He pointed to the chairs around his desk.

They sat down and started to look nervous. *Good,* he thought.

"Now," he said sitting in his chair and steepling his fingers. "How many of you had sex with Arnella Bancroft?"

The three of them were looking at each other nervously.

"Come on," Bancroft smiled at them coldly. "You must know that I know. You must know by now that she is my niece. If you didn't know, I am guessing you've heard what the trash paper printed this morning?"

"Er," Cory said shrugging, "I didn't."

"So you were the one who did the video?" Bancroft asked calmly. "The video that is now the hot topic of conversation?"

Cory cleared his throat. "It was Arnella's idea."

"Hogwash," Bancroft said still calm. "Now listen to me; I believe Arnella. Your little concocted story won't wash with me. So, either tell me the truth, or shut up. Who gave her the drugs?"

"There were no drugs," Jeff said, sweating. Dr. Bancroft was an imposing man and he looked as if he was tightly controlling his rage.

Bancroft growled. "I am not a violent man. Don't make me

shout. Here's the thing:" he said, leaning back in his chair, "I am going to expel the three of you effective immediately. I am also going to sue you for defamation of character. The police are going to find out who is the mastermind behind this little video scam and I am going to sue them too. If it's any of you, you had better speak up now. I am not in the mood for jokes. Chief Green is on standby to escort you all from this campus. You are banned from returning."

"My parents are going to kill me," Cory said, staring at Dr. Bancroft, scared. "I did not have sex with her; I only gave her the drugs. It was GHB. I just wanted to loosen her up a little, to make her relax with us. Arnella is always so uptight, and since high school she has been treating me like dirt."

Bancroft said softly, "Gamma-hydroxybutyric acid. How much did you give her?"

"It was just a capful," Cory said, "but it worked so fast on her and we had no idea...she would literally pass out so soon. That was not the reaction we wanted."

Bancroft bellowed. "A capful? Are you crazy? So, all three of you are Science majors? You deliberately carried a known central nervous system depressant which is known to increase sociability, promote libido and lower inhibitions to a party and gave a capful to an unknowing person?" He shook his head. "You know that overdosing on GHB can cause death?"

"Yes," Cory nodded vigorously. "At one point we thought we had killed her," Cory was trembling. "That's when I told David to stop, er stop what he was doing...she had passed out cold."

Bancroft swallowed the rage that was on the verge of spewing out of his mouth and looked at David who had hung his head.

"Anything to say for yourself David?"

David shook his head. "I am sorry. I didn't even finish having sex with her. I didn't mean it. I would give anything to take it back. The truth is Arnella is not a bad person and we just wanted to er..."

Bancroft winced. "And you Jeff, what was your roll in all of this? Oral sex with a drugged up girl?"

Jeff was sweating rivulets. His parents were prominent in the local community. He had just gone along for the ride when David and Cory mentioned what they were planning. He sighed. "I had nothing to do with any drugs, or any planning. Cory asked if I wanted to see a hot Arnella doing stuff and I said sure."

Bancroft nodded. "Okay. What about the video?"

The three of them looked at each other.

"We had dumped the SD card in deep trash," Cory said wiping his face. "We have no idea how it resurfaced."

Bancroft cleared his throat and then took up the phone. "Is that enough for you?"

"Yes," Natasha said at the door. "Thank you. You would make a formidable detective."

Behind her were three police officers and they all advanced towards the guys. "You are under arrest for the rape of Arnella Bancroft," Natasha said to the guys with a small smile on her lips.

"And you are expelled from this institution!" Bancroft growled emphatically.

Chapter Fourteen

Arnella spent a week vegetating in the basement. She painted picture after picture of torrid scenes. She only showered when she smelled herself and only ate when Charlene practically forced her to. She had regular visitors who tried to get her out of her doldrums. Her uncle was a regular visitor. He came with good news. The boys were in lock up. The gossip paper had printed a retraction, grovelling about how sorry they were for printing propaganda.

Jackie had dictated their exact statement. None of this news was enough to get a rise out of her flagging spirits. Taj and Natasha had both taken to visiting her at regular times. Kylie was like a shadow in the evenings, going so far as to take her computer and her husband to the basement where they camped out and tried to get her to talk.

She appreciated the show of love; she really did, but there was just a part of her that was incapable of appreciating it. Besides, she noticed the glaring absence of Alric, who wasn't calling or texting her or even responding to the rumors. That, more than anything else, was eating her up inside.

"You know what you need?" Charlene had stuck her head down the basement stairs. She was dressed in her gardening attire. "You need fresh air and sunlight. Exercise will make you feel better."

Arnella sighed. She was in a paint-splattered khaki shorts and a white t-shirt. "You may be right." She stretched and got up. "I am gonna take a walk down the road."

Charlene nodded. "I was thinking more about helping me and Micah in the greenhouse."

"Nah," Arnella said. "I want to be alone."

Charlene looked at her sympathetically. "Are you sure?"

"Quite sure." Arnella slipped on her battered sneakers and went up the stairs through the front door, down the garden and out onto the street. It was one of those evenings. The air was nippy and the sky was cloudy. She walked down the road slowly and tried to repress thoughts of Alric. What did he think of her now? She had not wanted to tell him about the video for the simple reason that she didn't want to have him thinking badly of her again. He had made her care about him and that made her feel even worse.

She was so focused on her thoughts that she never heard the car that pulled up beside her. It was only when the driver cleared his throat several times that she looked over. It was Alric. He looked sleepy, tousled, and so adorable to her.

"Hey," he said solemnly.

Arnella's heart jumped for joy. She inhaled deeply. "Hey yourself."

"I was interviewed by Natasha today," Alric said, sighing. "I am feeling a hell of a lot of guilt right now."

"Why?" Arnella asked curiously.

"I saw them surrounding you at the party." He smacked

his head with his open palm. "I was mad at them and you. I couldn't believe that you were laughing and cozying up to them like that. I was going to find you and give you a piece of my mind. God, I wish I had. I would have stopped this whole thing."

Arnella shrugged.

"So how are you feeling? I heard you weren't taking visitors."

"I am coming around," Arnella said, realizing that seeing Alric had lifted her spirits tremendously.

"So when are you coming back to school?" Alric asked.

"Maybe never." Arnella chuckled. "My uncle can't argue about that now."

Alric cleared his throat. "Want company on your walk?"

Arnella frowned. "I don't care."

Alric grinned. "That's Arnella speak for yes please. Can I park in your garage?"

Arnella nodded and watched as he drove off. She waited for him at the side of the road, her heart suddenly singing.

Suddenly things were not looking as bleak as they once were, and she found some of that fighting spirit that she had once prided herself on. Who knew that the missing ingredient all the while was Alric?

He jogged down to where she was standing and smiled. "I had a hellish week too."

"How so?" Arnella asked.

"Well, between studying for the interview, doing a final group project, and hearing that my friend was a porn star, things got pretty tough. Out of all of them, your news was pretty devastating. I got a video from EasterBunny too. To say that I was gobsmacked was an understatement."

"I really wish I knew who it was," Arnella said. In a hesitant voice, she asked, "Did you watch it?"

"Only the first part and only because I was in shock." Alric took her hand in his and squeezed them. "I deleted it."

"Thank you," Arnella said squeezing back his hand. "I can't remember most of what happened and I am grateful." She laughed uncomfortably. "That would have been my first time."

Alric stopped walking. "Ever. Are you saying? No wait a minute...Oh Lord," he groaned, "Arnella this is crazy. I am so sorry. They robbed you of what should have been a special moment by drugging you and then taping it?"

"Yup," Arnella smiled sadly. "I can genuinely say I don't remember my first time with a guy, or in my case, guys."

Alric was silent for a long time as they walked. They reached the intersection of Malvern, the sleepy town district. There was no one around. "Ready to turn back?" he asked.

"Sure." Arnella frowned at him. "You have gone silent."

"I am stupid." Alric shook his head. "I can't believe I listened to all the things about you. If I hadn't been as speedy to judge you, I could have saved you the trauma. I could have gotten to know you better. Things would have been different. I am so sorry." He stopped and looked at Arnella intently. "Please forgive me."

"The thought had not even occurred to me," Arnella said, "to blame you for anything. I can't forgive you. You did nothing wrong. For a time I liked being the notorious Arnella. You judged me as the town's bad girl. I judged you as the stuck up son of the pastor. We are even."

Alric grinned. "Me, stuck up?"

"Yup. Remember that night when Tracy introduced us? You looked down your nose at me."

"I was battling serious attraction," Alric said grinning, "and not to Tracy. You were in a red dress and you had your hair up in that sophisticated style that shows off your neck.

You seemed to look through me. I was mad as ever and really angry that I found you attractive."

They reached the house and Alric said softly. "I am relieved that you were not into that sex video willingly. The stress of it could have had me flunking this semester."

Arnella's heart fluttered uncomfortably.

"What I am trying to say here," Alric said, "and doing a bad job of it, is that I seriously like you. Like in a love kind of way... the kind that even sex videos of you with other men cannot kill. If it were any other girl, I would have written her off, but this week I couldn't write you off. I kept comparing the girl I think I know to the girl I saw in the video, and they were irreconcilable."

Arnella smiled, moving closer to Alric, "I like you too, in a love kind of way. This week, when I was dealing with the stress of being known as the schools porn star, my biggest problem was not hearing from you. What does that say?"

Alric chuckled. "It says that we have a thing for each other." He stepped closer to her. "Is it okay if I kiss you?"

Arnella nodded, dazed. His mouth came down on hers. His kiss was soft and gentle and exploratory. The imprint on her lips was like a new beginning, a benediction. It was okay; she was a woman, and alive. A low moan sounded in her throat and she closed her arms round him, stretching up on tiptoe to intensify their contact. He parted her velvety soft lips with his tongue.

They were so caught up in the experience that they didn't notice that they were being watched. The sound of a chuckle near them made her pull away from Alric and gasp in surprise.

It was Cathy Bancroft, Adrian's wife. "Sorry to intrude but it seems as if the kiss was going to go on for hours."

She laughed when Arnella hid her face in Adrian's chest.

"I came to extend a personal invitation to Natasha's

bachelorette party. It will be just us girls, two weeks from now, first week in November. It will be held here, at Deidra's. Deidra insisted. It will be a surprise."

She held out her hand to Alric, "I am Cathy. Can I tell you how marvelous it is to meet you? I was coming over here to keep my girl company only to find out she already has company."

Alric cleared his throat. "I am Alric Peterson."

"I know." Cathy giggled. "You play the organ at church. I am so happy to see Arnella in good company. Maybe now she will start attending church regularly."

"Shut up," Arnella said, still nestled in Alric's shirt.

Cathy chuckled. "I know when I am not wanted around. Remember the date and it's a surprise."

Arnella groaned when Cathy got into her car and tooted them. "Is she gone yet?"

Alric grinned. "You can look now... You are acting all shy."

Arnella looked up at him fiercely. "No, I am not. 'Shy' is not supposed to be in my vocabulary."

"So are we officially together," Alric asked, "or are we both still in denial?"

"Officially together." Arnella smiled, "I am so happy right now."

*****

"Iv'e never been to a bachelorette party," Kylie said, grinning at the punch bowl, "and I am glad I didn't look at what you guys got for Natasha: barely-there-lingerie and flavored condoms."

"What I can't believe," Natasha said grumpily, "is that Cathy wanted to invite Jackie Beecher."

"No," Deidra giggled, lying in one corner of the settee with her foot in Charlene's lap, "even though that would make the party really spicy. Jackie would make some droll observation, and Kylie or Natasha would wrestle her to the ground. Girl fight."

Natasha laughed. "In a weird way, I kind of like Jackie. She is the villain we love to hate."

Kylie snorted, coming to sit on the floor. "Not on your life. She was only living with Taj for a while and half heartedly tried to seduce him. She was married to my husband, and every chance she gets, she says in her sultry voice, 'Gareth remember when...' I can't believe how many memories she has stored in that brain of hers. I don't hate her but a polite distance is desired by all."

Arnella chuckled. She was enjoying the party. Her aunt Celeste had catered but didn't attend. Jessica was selecting music, sitting close to the laptop. Every song was her favorite, which of course was all Khaled. The other women in the family were chatting about their lives, their husbands, and their children. She loved it, the feeling of camaraderie and sisterhood. If she didn't have that video hanging over her head, she would declare the last two weeks the best of her life.

She saw Alric everyday, and they were connecting on a level that they had never quite attained before. They were truly friends. Her going back to school was drama free. People were more apologetic than gossipy. Maybe that had to do with the fact that her uncle had done an impassioned speech in general assembly on the dangers of rumors. He had hinted at the criminal nature of the boys' offence and how quick people were to judge. He had also had a medical student expound on the dangers of accepting drinks and foods from people they didn't know or trust, and the dangers of date rape.

Yes, it was shaping up to be a good two weeks.

"What are you over there grinning about, Nella?" Deidra asked lazily. "I heard that you have a boyfriend. Dish."

"Yes, Nella, dish." Natasha grinned. "Is it Pastor Peterson's son, Alric?"

Arnella looked at them and shook her head. "It's too early to dish. We have only just begun."

"Wooo," Cathy said breathily. "I think it is wonderful."

"Here here. Let's drink to that," Kylie giggled.

"Are you sure there is no alcohol in the punch?" Deidra asked, "Kylie seems tipsy."

Everybody laughed.

Chapter Fifteen

"**Y**ou look happy today." Taj observed Arnella, who was sitting in his recliner with a pleased smile on her face. "Want to tell me about it?"

Arnella grinned. "It was a great bachelorette party last night. Totally good. I had quite forgotten how pleasant family gatherings could be."

Taj smiled, "Natasha told me you guys had a great time."

Arnella said dreamily, "Yes, we did. I love December weddings. Natasha said you guys are thinking about Lovers Leap. You should totally get married there. It is a gorgeous location with the sea as backdrop and that plunging vertical drop."

"I love the location too," Taj said. "The time is not really my choosing. My Dad will be on vacation then. I had to take that into consideration."

"I sometimes forget that you have two Dads. How does that feel?"

"Ah," Taj grinned, "spending too much time with me? You are asking me the feeling questions."

Arnella giggled. "Sorry. "

"I don't think of Ryan Bancroft as my Dad, well, not really." Taj said, "He's shaping up to be a good friend though. Let's talk about you. Are you sleeping better?"

"Yes," Arnella nodded. "I haven't received anymore videos. I feel really lighter since the guys are not on campus. Natasha said I will have to testify at their trial."

"How do feel about that?" Taj asked looking at her closely.

"I never imagined that there would have been justice with this whole thing, so I am fine with where it's at now."

"So how is Alric?" Taj asked.

"He's wonderful." Arnella giggled. "I feel like a girl around him…a totally wimpy female. I hate the feeling but love it at the same time."

"And Tracy? When last have you seen her?"

"I haven't seen her since that time she showed up at Alric's apartment. I think she's mad at me or something, which is ridiculous. I think I should be the one mad at her. She calls herself a friend and yet she told the most vicious lies about me."

"How do you feel about her?" Taj asked.

"I don't miss her, and her so called friendship." Arnella closed her eyes. "I had the ugliest thing happen to me at her house, and she didn't care. She said I was hallucinating. Imagine that. She was probably glad that this happened. Maybe it is some form of consolation for her that I was assaulted at her place, who knows?"

*****

Natasha sat around her desk at her apartment; finishing her

final project. Her desk was piled high with papers, jottings, and post it notes. She was on her way to becoming a master's degree graduate in Forensic Psychology, plus she had a wedding in just four weeks, and she still had that unresolved case of Arnella's sitting above her head. She had three separate white boards, which she called her sane boards, so that she could track the three important events in her life.

She was itching to solve the case of who was behind the videos that were sent to Arnella. So far, only Arnella, the two guys from the gossip paper, and Alric had received videos.

She glanced at the board that she had peppered with the photos of everybody at the party. It had taken her a while to find them in order to ask them if they knew about the SD card. She looked at Tracy's photo again. Her eyes kept wandering back to her.

She resented Arnella for stealing Alric from her. She had motive to be sending those videos. She had interviewed Tracy before, but she had this niggling feeling that she knew something. Natasha glanced at her project then at her watch. She needed to talk to Tracy again.

***** *

Tracy was in the Business Center with a group of her law school pals when Natasha called. She picked up the phone and rolled her eyes. "Annoying detective," she said to her friends before answering. They snickered as she answered the phone pleasantly.

"Hello, Tracy, it's me Natasha Rowe. Can I meet with you? There is something that is on my mind."

Tracy flashed her hair over shoulders and said firmly, "It is my constitutional right not to have meetings with detectives if I don't want to. I have told you all I know. I have no idea who has been distributing videos of Arnella Bancroft. I certainly didn't do it. Now please leave me alone."

Her group of friends cheered when she hung up the phone.

"I hope that takes care of that," Tracy said haughtily. "As if I would stoop so low as to care who Arnella has sex with. I hope the boys have a good lawyer so that they can get off from this nonsense. You saw her at my party; did she look like somebody who was being drugged?"

The group laughed. There were three girls and two guys in the group. However, one of the girls, Sandrina shook her head. "What you are saying is wrong Tracy. Where is your sympathy? You are a woman. Would you like something like that to happen to you? I don't endorse what you are saying."

Tracy rolled her eyes. "If you knew Arnella like I did, you would not be taking up for her. She deserves everything she got and more."

Sandrina shook her head. "I can't agree with you on that one."

*****

It was the first week in December, and classes were ending. Exams were just around the corner. Arnella had her final lab with Alric; she was just leaving class when he detained her.

"Remember that the Med Association Fundraiser is tomorrow night," Alric said, "You haven't shown me which one of your paintings you are going to donate."

Arnella pondered that. "I am not going to show you either. I don't want you to hate it. I have severe artist sensitivity."

Alric chuckled. "I have your ticket right here with me. The Fundraiser this year will be in the President's Ballroom. This year we invited all the moneyed people that we could get contacts for."

"Sounds intimidating," Arnella grinned. "I'll just drop off the painting and disappear."

"No you don't," Alric said, "I want you to be there. I have a class and then I'll just change and meet you there. Come an hour earlier so that we can set up your painting. It's a date. Sorry I can't collect you and hand you flowers like in the movies." He kissed her on the lips, "And dress formally."

"I'll have to raid Deidra's closet."

"Wear red." Alric winked. "You look lovely in red."

Arnella pondered. Deidra had her closet color-coded, so red and all its shades shouldn't be too hard to find. "Talk to you later?"

"Sure," Alric said, "I'll be in the Med Library."

Arnella headed out of the classroom, thinking to herself which painting would be the most appropriate…the one that would make the most impact. Then of course she thought of the scene with the driftwood. It was done in oil. It was glorious, in her opinion, but as usual, she felt weird putting it on display for the world to see.

*****

Arnella arrived at the president's building in a red dress. Deidra had given her carte blanche to her closet. "Take whatever you want," Deidra had said when she called to ask. The whole closet is yours, if you want it.

Arnella had stood in the huge space, not knowing what to do. She had chosen a blood red dress, which was simple and elegant, and she had swept her hair up in the style that Alric liked.

The ballroom was decorated in pure white. She had the painting in her hand; a girl with "Usher" emblazoned on her jacket came up to her. "May I help you?"

"This is supposed to be for auction." Arnella indicated to the painting. "Where should I put it?"

"Oh, Arnella Bancroft," the girl said brightly. "I am Maria. Come this way. Alric said you would be early."

She walked toward a stage area, looking behind at Arnella. "We have five big ticket items for auction tonight. There is a dinner date for two with the President."

"Seriously," Arnella grinned. "People will bid to go out with my uncle?"

"He's well respected in the business world," Maria grinned. "Then there is a weekend for two at Sandals, Turks and Caicos."

"I'd take that!" Arnella nodded. "Definitely."

"Then there are two tickets to the track and field finals at the Olympics in France next year. Marcus Bancroft hooked us up. There are also two concert tickets and a back stage pass to a Khaled concert in Kingston."

"Oh man," Arnella shook her head. "If my cousin, Jessica, heard this she'd probably get her parents in trouble by bidding millions to get that ticket."

Maria shook her head. "She's not alone. Anyway, your painting is the fifth high-ticket item. Alric said he hasn't seen it."

She looked doubtful as she indicated to the easel. "We were desperate for a fifth item though, so we trusted him about this."

Arnella sighed. "He doesn't even know which painting I was going to bring."

Maria blanched. "You mean he has never seen your work before?"

"No," Arnella said, taking off the covering and putting it on the easel.

"Whoa!" Maria said, looking at the picture. "It is gorgeous.

You did this?" She was looking from the painting to Arnella in awe.

"Yes," Arnella said humbly. "You like it? Does it fit being a big ticket item?"

"Does it fit?" Maria was shaking her head. "It's gorgeous. It's oil paint? It has a glow."

"Yes," Arnella said. "I had to do it in oil for the sea to have some movement. Watercolors don't do nearly as good a job as oil does for movement, and I had to do a number of layers to get the sea to look alive. I don't like the effect acrylic gives me when I do it in layers."

Maria shook her head. "This is going to be the biggest seller here. I wish I could afford to bid on it."

Arnella smiled. She had sudden pangs about giving it away herself. It had been her catharsis; the painting had been therapy. All her emotions went into it, and it showed.

"I am serious." Maria went up to the painting. "It looks real, and every time I look at it I get a different feeling."

She stood in front of the painting for so long that Arnella left her to it and looked around. They were going to have a live band. The band was setting up and doing mike tests. The piano player was already playing some tunes and Arnella bopped her head to his selections.

Maria turned to her. "You are going to be famous."

Arnella nodded. "I don't want fame, just the opportunity to paint, and be happy, and to be loved, and to love, and to..."

"Marry Alric and have his children and to go to heaven with Alric and said children." Alric said behind her.

Arnella looked around and gasped.

Maria smiled. "Sounds like a plan. I have everything covered here. You can go have fun until the auction."

Alric nodded and grinned down at Arnella and then looked at the painting. "I knew it."

"You knew what?"

"I knew that you were creative and passionate and troubled. I hear that is what makes the best paintings. This is gorgeous. And you used oil, like the old masters."

He hugged her tightly. "I picked winners, both girl and painting, and didn't even know it."

Arnella hugged him back. "I hope it gets a good price at your auction."

Alric grinned. "I can't wait to see how this will go. By the way, you look simply beautiful."

"You do too." Arnella said drinking him in with her eyes. "You clean up pretty well."

Alric grinned. Before he could respond, a group of persons, led by Maria, gathered around the painting and swamped Arnella with questions about it.

*****

The party started promptly at seven. There was dinner at eight, and the auction began at nine. Alric had secured her a seat with him at dinner. Arnella bumped into her Aunt Celeste and Uncle Ryan.

Celeste gave her a big hug. "I saw your painting. You need to do something for me. I can't have a niece with this much talent and not have an early piece at home."

Arnella grinned. "Yes ma'am."

Her uncle squeezed her affectionately. "I am proud of you."

"Thanks, Uncle Ryan." She kissed him on the cheek. They didn't chitchat for long because he was in demand.

She looked around for Alric and saw him standing in a corner with Tracy, a heavily made up, beautiful Tracy in a flattering peach dress. She was standing with her father.

Arnella dithered about going over. She looked away from them and her eyes met Natasha's. She waved. Natasha walked over to her. "You look lovely." She hugged Arnella. "I love your painting. I can't bid. Even if I could, I would be outbidded. I hear rich people talking about it. They are really excited."

Arnella laughed. "So, why are you here? If not to auction."

"Because Taj is here," Natasha said. "He got tickets to it. He thought I should play dress up for an evening. We rarely have any social events to go to up here in the hills."

Arnella nodded, "That's true."

"So, that's Miss Tracy Carr? Dressed to the nines, huh." Natasha said nodding in Tracy's direction.

"Yes," Arnella said, "and the big bulldog man beside her is her doting papa."

"Let us go and say hi," Natasha said putting on her detective face.

"No," Arnella said vigorously. "You are not here to work but to party."

"You are right," Natasha said regretfully, "but I would just love to see how Tracy behaves when she is around her Dad, and Alric. She is a tough cookie you know. I got a hint of that the other day when I called her."

"Okay let's go over," Arnella sighed. "But be warned, Mr. Carr hates me."

"Mr. Carr looks like he has a chip on those broad beefy shoulders," Natasha said walking with Arnella over to the group.

"Hello," Natasha said brightly, "Mr. Carr, Tracy."

"Hello," Mr. Carr looked at Arnella and twisted his lips. He looked back at Natasha, putting on a social smile. "I didn't get your name."

"Natasha Rowe," Natasha said brightly, "I am a student

here and part time detective, working with the police force."

Mr. Carr looked at Tracy uncomfortably. "That's interesting."

"And of course, here is my girlfriend, Arnella," Alric said, taking her hands and dragging her to his side.

Mr. Carr sniffed. "I know her."

"Yes he does," Arnella said, grinning. "The last time I was at his house he cussed me to high heaven."

Tracy flicked a hunk of hair over her shoulders. "That's because you deserved it."

Arnella nodded. "I see."

"Well, it was nice meeting you Alric." Mr. Carr shook his hand and walked away. Tracy walked behind him, looking back at Arnella with venom in her gaze, and then at Alric longingly.

Natasha was shaking with laughter. "What on earth did you do to that man that was so bad, Arnella? He is treating you as if you have leprosy."

Arnella shrugged. "Who knows what his darling Tracy told him about me. Boy, was I duped into believing that she was my friend."

*****

The dinner was a lively affair. Alric had placed them around a table with some of his fellow medical students and two prominent surgeons who were hilarious and down to earth. Arnella was enjoying their company even though she had initially thought that she would have been bored to death and would have a terrible time.

After dinner, the auction began and the auctioneer read out the items that were up for bidding. She had told Alric not to reveal her name to the crowd; she wanted her work to speak for itself, and so when the auctioneer said, "A painting by AB," she smiled wildly.

Alric squeezed her hand. The bidding began with the tickets for the Olympics. The bidding was intense and was "Spurred on by the wives," Alric said to her gleefully.

She was enjoying the back and forth as persons raised their paddles and quoted increasingly huge sums. She was tickled pink when her Uncle was bidded on for over a hundred thousand dollars. He had straightened his tie, and was looking uncomfortable as more and more sums piled up for him. Finally, one portly old lady got him for $150,000.

Arnella chuckled. When her uncle saw who it was, he looked as if he had bitten a lemon. Her Aunt Celeste was looking very pleased.

When it was time for her painting, the auctioneer had it brought onto the stage and the bidding began in earnest.

"Let's start the bidding at $50, 000," the auctioneer said. Quickly it was driven up to $150,000 then $300, 000. Then there was an outright war between two bidders.

"I can't believe this," Alric said, whispering to Arnella fiercely, who had her eyes firmly fixed on the floor. She couldn't look. "Tracy's father is bidding like mad on your painting."

Arnella turned around swiftly and realized that he indeed was, along with an older gentleman with a white moustache. The older gentleman finally won at $400,000.

Arnella was shell-shocked. Her painting sold for $400, 000! She kept pinching her hand to feel if she was dreaming. It was obvious that Mr. Carr hadn't known that the painting was hers.

She felt lightheaded and readily got up with Alric to dance to the socially conscious song "Wake Up Everybody" by Teddy Prendergass.

She twirled and swung on the dance floor, laughing at Alric's dance moves. In mid laugh, she looked over her shoulder to see a scowling Mr. Carr talking to a smiling Natasha. She touched Alric's hand. "I bet Natasha just told him that he had bidded on my painting." Alric laughed.

"I think tonight is ranking right up there with my best moments in life," Arnella said brightly.

Chapter Sixteen

Natasha handed in her final assignment at the Forensic lab and was heading out of the building, a light feeling to her steps. She had accomplished one of her three major tasks. She went over the checklist in her head: *Master's project— check, Arnella's sex video mystery—to solve, get married to the love of my life—definitely can't wait to check.*

She hadn't called Miles for the past three days. She dialed his number, crossing her fingers mentally and hoping that he would have good news for her.

"Yo, Tasha. What's up?" Miles answered.

"You know what I am calling for," Natasha said. "Please, please tell me you have the address."

"I do," Miles said.

"Yes," Natasha squealed. She stopped at her car.

"Who is it?"

"The person who signed up for the account is first name, Easter. Last name Bunny."

"You have got to be kidding me." Natasha ran her hand through her hair frustratedly.

"Address: 115 North Never Never Land," Miles continued, "age 85."

"No." Natasha sighed. "They used a bogus name and address to sign up for the account."

"Yup, that's what people do when they don't want to be found." Miles laughed. "However, based on the IP address that the mail was sent from, the general area where the email was sent from is Santa Cruz, Jamaica."

"Oh no." Natasha groaned. "I waited all this time for this. Santa Cruz, Jamaica has over two hundred thousand people living there. The party was there. It could be anybody."

"Don't worry about it," Miles said. "The person sent a message on the second week in November from their telephone."

"What does that mean?" Natasha asked.

"It means that the meta data that is stored on the phone contains information on which cell phone towers were used. I took the liberty of calling the cell phone provider of the phone, and they deduced that the cell phone tower closest to where the mail was sent is at Cherry Hill."

"But that's exactly where the party was." Natasha groaned.

"Well that's where the culprit is," Miles said.

"Thanks, Miles," Natasha said, "I owe you one."

"Dinner?" Miles asked smoothly.

"I am getting married in a week." Natasha laughed. "Sorry, no dinner."

"Bummer," Miles said goodnaturedly. "All the best with your marriage. He's not a fellow officer is he?"

"No," Natasha said, "and Thanks."

She hung up the phone and pondered her options. The person who sent the video lived in Cherry Hill. She could have bet her bottom dollar that it had been Tracy. She had wanted it to be Tracy. She had thought the girl obnoxious and snide, especially after that last phone call when she had snarkily cut her off.

She had wanted to charge her with being an accessory to a crime and watch the fear leech into her eyes. Now, she was back to square one. She called Tony Beaker to see if he was available for a ride to Cherry Hill. She would just have to go to the Carr's house and bluff her way through.

*****

When Natasha and Tony reached the Carr's, darkness had just fallen. They had had to wait almost three hours to get a search warrant for the computers in the house and Natasha had to justify to the Assistant Supe why she would be doing such a thing to a prominent banker, but she remembered the way that Frederick Carr had sneered at Arnella.

The nearer they got to the house, the more she was convinced that he might have found the video and hated her enough to be tormenting her with it.

The house was located at the top of a hill overlooking the town. There was an automatic gate, and she pressed the buzzer.

"Who is it?" a disembodied voice asked.

"Natasha Rowe and Tony Beaker from Mount Faith. We have a search warrant for the computers, and computer and video related technology belonging to Frederick Carr and Cathlyn Carr."

They waited four minutes before the gate swung open. "A livid Cathlyn Carr stood on the veranda.

"What is the meaning of this, officers?"

"A crime was committed here on your property, the rape

and subsequent video taping of Arnella Bancroft." Natasha said, pushing her hand in her jeans. "We have evidence to believe that videos which the boys taped and threw away were sent from this house."

Cathlyn had her hands akimbo. "I can't let you search my husband's laptop till he gets home. He didn't carry it to work today. He is a banker. You can always search mine."

Natasha shook her head. "We can't wait on him to get here, so you'd better alert him that we are here."

Cathlyn shrugged. "Sure. I am sure you are barking up the wrong tree. How is Arnella? I remembered thinking that something was definitely off with her that morning."

"She's doing great," Natasha said. "The boys confessed their misdeeds on video and are set for trial in the new year."

"Good," Cathlyn said feelingly. "I am happy that she is getting justice. I am really sorry that it happened here too."

Natasha looked at Tony. She did not seem like the kind of person to mess with Arnella, but they still had to check. She handed them her laptop and her husband's.

"Are these all the computers in the house?" Natasha asked.

"Yes," Cathlyn said. "That's it. When can I get it back, I have a presentation on it that should be delivered three days from now?"

"Tomorrow morning at the Malvern station," Natasha said, "provided that there is no evidence related to the case."

Cathlyn shrugged. "I am sure there is none for either me or Fred."

She saw them out and Natasha and Tony drove to the station. Natasha was deep in thought. "Who else could it be?" she asked Tony. "I am at my wits end trying to figure this one out."

"I would love to know too," Tony said. They headed to his office as soon as they arrived at the station and powered up the computers.

Natasha looked through Frederick Carr's computer first, going straight to his video files.

Tony did the same to Cathlyn's computer. There were no video files on Cathlyn's but quite a few on Fredericks. There were parties, bootleg movies, several clips of half naked girls, and there it was: the big uncut file with Arnella.

Natasha sat down hard on the chair behind her. "Eureka!" she squealed. "We have our guy. Our dear Frederick Carr is either some kind of a perv or he really really disliked Arnella."

She looked on the clock on the bare office walls. It was eight o'clock. "Just one week now to go for my wedding Tony. This is another check on my list."

"What are we to charge him with?" Tony asked.

"Failure to report a crime? The uncut video shows what was really happening here. Look at the ending." She pointed to the screen.

Arnella had stopped breathing. She was passed out cold and the guys were trying to revive her. David snarled, "Turn the camera off."

Jeff was looking frightened. "Destroy it. She's dead. Oh my God she's dead." The screen went blank.

Natasha said, "He didn't report it. He edited the thing and tried to torment Arnella with it by sending it to a gossip paper and then to a guy she liked. This man must have the brain of a ten year old boy."

"You are insulting ten year old boys," Tony said ruefully.

"I know." Natasha got up. "I am sorry. Throw the book at him. Find out where the original file is and get him to hand it over. Destroy all the copies. Give this guy hell."

"Wait a minute," Tony said, "You can't just leave now. He'll be here in no time with his guilty self. Don't you want to know the motive for this?"

Natasha shrugged and then sat down. "Okay, why not?"

*****

She didn't have long to wait. Frederick Carr burst into the station with his lawyer, a well-fed guy in pants that were too tight. He was trailing Frederick in a huff. An officer showed them to Tony's office, and he came through the door, a storm cloud over his face.

"How dare you take my computer without permission?"

Natasha laughed. "How dare you? That should be my question Mr. Carr. Read the man his rights Tony."

"Just hold on a minute," Frederick Carr said, suddenly frightened.

Tony got up. "You are really making our jobs easier for us. Frederick Carr, you are charged with failure to report a crime in the rape of Arnella Bancroft, and possession of bootleg copyrighted materials. You have the right to remain silent..."

Natasha smiled, mainly because Frederick Carr had come to a sputtering halt. His lawyer listened impatiently to the reading of the rights and muttered. "This is rubbish, Fred. I can straighten this up in no time."

Fred was nodding like a bobble doll, guilt weighing heavy on his face.

"Why did you do it?" Natasha asked, "I am simply asking. There is no need to have your lawyer tell you not to answer; we have the evidence on your machine."

"I don't know how it got there," Frederick said, "This is ridiculous."

"Who else uses your computer Mr. Carr?" Natasha asked. "Your daughter perhaps?"

"Leave her out of this," Frederick bellowed. "She had

nothing to do with any of this. She is not friends with that slutty girl, Arnella, anymore."

"I know Tracy had nothing to do with this," Natasha said, " You see, I figured it out. All the times when the videos were sent, they were sent from Cherry Hill. She was up here, at Mount Faith. Why'd you hate Arnella so? She is a girl the same age as your daughter and you took painstaking time to edit these videos done by those boys and torment her with them and tried to spread it around the school? It must have really pained your heart when you found out that she did that picture that you were bidding on, that gorgeous picture reflecting her pain."

Natasha shook her head. "I hope you serve time for this. I've gotta go, Tony. Book him." She got up from the chair. At the least she knew that Frederick Carr would get a sleepover in jail because there was no processing after six.

*****

Arnella was in the Medical Library with Alric and his batch mates. They had roped her in as an interviewer in their mock up to the mini interview. She covered a large yawn with her hand. Twice Kim had pinched her to stay awake as she asked them question after question about ethical considerations. She listened to their responses and then argued with some of them. They were enjoying her refreshing take on the issues, when her phone rang.

"Mystery solved," Natasha said to Arnella. "Your video sender Easter Bunny is actually Frederick Carr, banker, family man, and currently in our jail overnight."

"I can't believe it." Arnella whispered. "Then again, it doesn't surprise me. He was really against me and Tracy being friends. They are very close. I don't even want to think of what she told him. It now makes sense that Alric was the only one, besides myself who got a copy of the video."

"That's right," Natasha said solemnly. "He was doing this to discredit you at the school, and with Alric, to please his daughter. Probably thought he would never get caught. The videos will be destroyed after the court case so that they will never haunt you again."

"Thank God," Arnella said, with feeling.

"Can you give me an alternate number for Vanley. He is going to be officiating in the wedding next week Sunday. I want to do a rehearsal on Saturday night."

"Sure," Arnella rolled off a number from the top of her head. "Thanks, Natasha," she said softly.

"You are more than welcome. You got your invite right? I am guessing your plus one is Alric."

"Yes. Definitely. Could be nobody else." Arnella hung up the phone and went back to the group, smiling. She hugged Alric around his neck and whispered. "I love you."

Alric looked at her warmly. "I love you too, Nella, every bit of you."

The End

Here's a Look at the Next Book in the Series:

A Younger Man

"If anyone knows of any reason these two should not be married, speak now or forever hold your peace."

The place was silent, except for the rustling of the wind on the red and white streamers that were pinned to each chair and a seagull squawking in the distance. Vanley Bancroft grinned with the bride and groom in front of him, who were not concerned about the possibility of any objection coming from the audience. They only had eyes for each other.

"Taj Jackson and Natasha Rowe, I now declare you husband and wife. You may kiss your bride, sir."

Taj lowered his head to Natasha and kissed her thoroughly, a kiss which went on an on, and had their one hundred and twenty guests laughing and clapping.

Vanley breathed a sigh of relief. It was over: his first wedding as an officiating minister. He had not made a blunder, and he was happy. He had made a terrible blunder at his first funeral. Even now, he shuddered to think of it. He kept on calling the deceased Anita Parkinson when the name was Agnes Bertrand.

One lady had taken him aside after the funeral and asked curiously if Anita Parkinson wasn't the VP of Academic Affairs at Mount Faith. Vanley had been shocked to his core. His obsession with Anita had gotten so bad that he had been calling her name in a funeral service, of all things!

Today, he had taken extra precautions. He had tried not to think about Anita, which was hard because she was a guest at the wedding, sitting at the back in a flirty blue dress and a blue hat that she was constantly holding down because of the breeze. He had registered all these details and knew every time she raised one of her hands to keep the hat down. Her nails were painted a pretty coral blue. He even knew every time she swallowed in the last half hour. When Taj and Natasha walked to the end of the gazebo with a saxophone rendition of John Legend's song "Stay With You" playing in the background, Vanley gave Pastor Peterson a parting handshake and stepped down from the gazebo. He zeroed in on Anita, but she was engaged in animated conversation with his cousin, Kylie, and her husband, Gareth.

He walked to the side of the lawn instead and gazed toward the sea. It was a beautiful spot for a wedding; Taj and Natasha had chosen well. The venue was called Lovers Leap and had a legend attached to it. Two slave lovers from the 18th century fled to the edge of the large steep cliff while being chased by the plantation owner. Rather than face being caught and separated, the pair chose to end their lives by jumping together. In previous years, when Vanley had heard the story, he had scoffed at their drastic action, but today, with the cool December breeze swirling around and the romantic ambience of the wedding, and his unshakeable obsession with Anita, he could see how a couple would rather die than be separated.

"You did well today."

Vanley swiveled around and saw that it was her. She had taken off the hat, and her hair, which she kept in a sleek bob, was swinging toward her face. She had a heart shaped face and the biggest, sultriest brown eyes this side of Jamaica.

"Thank you," he smiled.

He always smiled when she was around. Usually, he felt like a bumbling idiot and would blurt out something totally inappropriate.

Last time it was, "Marry me, Anita." Today, he straightened his spine and kept his mouth shut.

Her response last time was to laugh at him. "You are too young for me, Vanley."

He was tired of her keeping him at arms length. Fifteen years was not that big a deal...

OTHER BOOKS BY BRENDA BARRETT

Love Triangle Series

Love Triangle: Three Sides To The Story - George, the husband, Marie, the wife and Karen-the mistress. They all get to tell their side of the story.

Love Triangle: After The End -Torn between two lovers. Colleen married her high school sweetheart, Isaiah, hoping that they would live happily ever after but life intruded and Isaiah disappeared at sea. She found work with the rich and handsome, Enrique Lopez, as a housekeeper and realized that she couldn't keep him at arms length...

Love Triangle: On The Rebound - For Better or Worse, Brandon vowed to stay with Ashley, but when worse got too much he moved out and met Nadine. For the first time in years he felt happy, but then Ashley remembered her wedding vows...

New Song Series

Going Solo (New Song Series-Book 1) - Carson Bell, had a lovely voice, a heart of gold, and was no slouch in the looks department. So why did Alice abandon him and their daughter? What did she want after ten years of silence?

Duet on Fire (New Song Series-Book 2) - Ian and Ruby had problems trying to conceive a child. If that wasn't enough, her ex-lover the current pastor of their church wants her back...

Tangled Chords (New Song Series-Book 3) - Xavier Bell, the poor, ugly duckling has made it rich and his looks have been incredibly improved too. Farrah Knight, hotel heiress had cruelly rejected him in the past but now she needed help. Could Xavier forgive and forget?

Broken Harmony (New Song Series-Book 4) - Aaron Lee, wanted the top job in his family company but he had a moral clause to consider just when Alka, his married ex-girlfriend walks back into his life.

A Past Refrain (New Song Series-Book 5) - Jayce had issues with forgetting Haley Greenwald even though he had a new woman in his life. Will he ever be able to shake his love for Haley?

Perfect Melody (New Song Series-Book 6) - Logan Moore had the perfect wife, Melody but his secretary Sabrina was hell bent on breaking up the family. Sabrina wanted Logan whatever the cost and she had a secret about Melody, that could shatter Melody's image to everyone.

The Bancroft Family Series

Homely Girl (The Bancrofts-Book 0) - April and Taj were opposites in so many ways. He was the cute, athletic boy that everybody wanted to be friends with. She was the overweight, shy, and withdrawn girl. Do April and Taj have a love that can last a lifetime? Or will time and separate paths rip them apart?

Saving Face (The Bancrofts-Book 1) - Mount Faith

University drama begins with a dead president and several suspects including the president in waiting Ryan Bancroft.

Tattered Tiara (The Bancrofts-Book 2) - Micah Bancroft is targeted by femme fatale Deidra Durkheim. There are also several rape cases to be solved.

Private Dancer (The Bancrofts-Book 3) - Adrian Bancroft was gutted when he returned to Jamaica and found out that his first and only love Cathy Taylor was a stripper and was literally owned by the menacing drug lord, Nanjo Jones.

Goodbye Lonely (The Bancrofts-Book 4) - Kylie Bancroft was shy and had to resort to going to confidence classes. How could she win the love of Gareth Beecher, her faculty adviser, a man with a jealous ex-wife in his past and a current mystery surrounding a hand found in his garden?

Practice Run (The Bancrofts Book 5) - Marcus Bancroft had many reasons to avoid Mount Faith but Deidra Durkheim was not one of them. Unfortunately, on one of his visits he was the victim of a deliberate hit and run.

Sense of Rumor (The Bancrofts-Book 6) - Arnella Bancroft was the wild, passionate Bancroft, the creative loner who didn't mind living dangerously; but when a terrible thing happened to her at her friend Tracy's party, it changed her. She found that courting rumors can be devastating and that only the truth could set her free.

A Younger Man (The Bancrofts- Book 7) - Pastor Vanley Bancroft loved Anita Parkinson despite their fifteen-year age gap, but Anita had a secret, one that she could not reveal to Vanley. To tell him would change his feelings toward her, or force him to give up the ministry that he loved so much.

Just To See Her (The Bancrofts- Book 8) - Jessica Bancroft had the opportunity to meet her fantasy guy Khaled, he was finally coming to Mount Faith but she had feelings for Clay Reid, a guy who had all the qualities she was looking for. Who would she choose and what about the weird fascination Khaled had for Clay?

The Three Rivers Series

Private Sins (Three Rivers Series-Book 1) - Kelly, the first lady at Three Rivers Church was pregnant for the first elder of her church. Could she keep the secret from her husband and pretend that all was well?

Loving Mr. Wright (Three Rivers Series-Book 2) - Erica saw one last opportunity to ditch her single life when Caleb Wright appeared in her town. He was perfect for her, but what was he hiding?

Unholy Matrimony (Three Rivers Series-Book 3) - Phoebe had a problem, she was poor and unhappy. Her solution to marry a rich man was derailed along the way with her feelings for Charles Black, the poor guy next door.

If It Ain't Broke (Three Rivers Series-Book 4) - Chris Donahue wanted a place in his child's life. Pinky Black just wanted his love. She also wanted him to forget his obsession with Kelly and love her. That shouldn't be so hard? Should it?

Contemporary Romance/Drama

The Preacher And The Prostitute - Prostitution and the clergy don't mix. Tell that to ex-prostitute, Maribel, who finds herself in love with the Pastor at her church. Can an ex-prostitute and a pastor have a future together?

New Beginnings - Inner city girl Geneva was offered an opportunity of a lifetime when she found out that her 'real' father was a very wealthy man. Her decision to live up-town meant that she had to leave Froggie, her 'ghetto don,' behind. She also found herself battling with her stepmother and battling her emotions for Justin, a suave up-towner.

Full Circle - After graduating from university, Diana wanted to return to Jamaica to find her siblings. What she didn't foresee was that she would meet Robert Cassidy and that both their pasts would be intertwined, and that disturbing questions would pop up about their parentage, just when they were getting close.

Historical Fiction/Romance

The Empty Hammock - Workaholic, Ana Mendez, fell asleep in a hammock and woke up in the year 1494. It was the time of the Tainos, a time when life seemed simpler, but Ana knew that all of that was about to change.

The Pull Of Freedom - Even in bondage the people, freshly arrived from Africa, considered themselves free. Led by Nanny and Cudjoe the slaves escaped the Simmonds' plantation and went in different directions to forge their destiny in the new country called Jamaica.

Jamaican Comedy (Material contains Jamaican dialect)

Di Taxi Ride And Other Stories - Di Taxi Ride and Other Stories is a collection of twelve witty and fast paced short stories. Each story tells of a unique slice of Jamaican life.

CPSIA information can be obtained at www.ICGtesting.com
Printed in the USA
LVOW06s2134260715

447744LV00008B/60/P